The Messiah of Stockholm

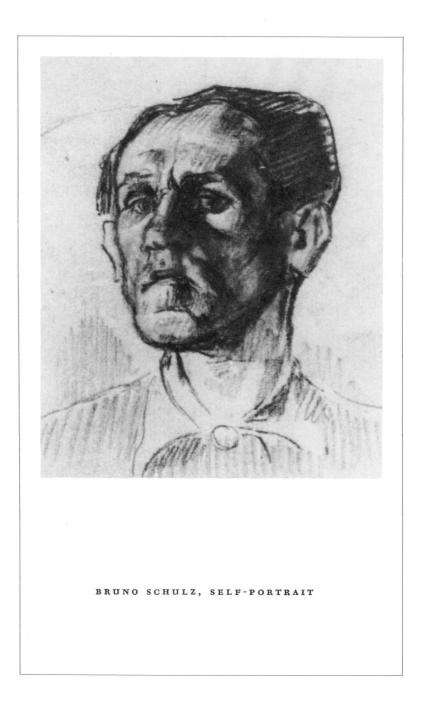

BRUNO SCHULZ, SELF-PORTRAIT

The Messiah
of Stockholm

A NOVEL BY

Cynthia Ozick

ALFRED A. KNOPF

NEW YORK 1987

THIS IS A BORZOI BOOK
PUBLISHED BY ALFRED A. KNOPF, INC.

Copyright © 1987 by Cynthia Ozick

Library of Congress Cataloging-in-Publication Data
Ozick, Cynthia.
The Messiah of Stockholm.
1. Schulz, Bruno, 1892-1942, in fiction, drama,
poetry, etc. I. Title.
PS3565.Z5M4 1987 813'.54 86-46014
ISBN 0-394-54701-2

Manufactured in the United States of America
First Edition

TO
PHILIP ROTH

My father never tired of glorifying this extraordinary element—matter.

"There is no dead matter," he taught us, "lifelessness is only a disguise behind which hide unknown forms of life. The range of these forms is infinite and their shades and nuances limitless. The Demiurge was in possession of important and interesting creative recipes. Thanks to them, he created a multiplicity of species which renew themselves by their own devices. No one knows whether these recipes will ever be reconstructed. But this is unnecessary, because even if the classical methods of creation should prove inaccessible for evermore, there still remain some illegal methods, an infinity of heretical and criminal methods."

Bruno Schulz, *The Street of Crocodiles*

Jag är stjärnan som speglar sig i dig.
. . .
Din själ är mitt hem. Jag har inget annat.

I am the star that mirrors itself in you.
. . .
Your soul is my home. I have no other.

Pär Lagerkvist, *Aftonland*
(Translated by W. H. Auden and Leif Sjöberg)

The Messiah of Stockholm

1

AT THREE in the afternoon—the hour when, all over the world, the literary stewpot boils over, when gossip in the book-reviewing departments of newspapers is most untamed and swarming, and when the autumn sky over Stockholm begins to draw down a translucent dusk (an eggshell shielding a blue-black yolk) across the spired and watery town—at this lachrymose yet exalted hour, Lars Andemening could be found in bed, napping. Not that there was anyone to look for him there. He had no wife; his apartment was no bigger than a crack in the wall, and any visitor a biennial event; and the quilt, heaped on itself in large knots, was a risen tangle that might or might not have hinted at the presence of Lars under it. As it happened, he was there nearly every afternoon from November to early in a certain bare and harrowing March, when he gave it up; but no one knew.

He lived a ten-minute walk from the *Morgontörn*, his employer—a relatively young newspaper of unsettled character, in competition for the morning trade with the majestic old *Dagens Nyheter* and the respectable *Svenska Dagbladet*. Lars himself was, at least in appearance, relatively young; he was forty-two and looked much younger, probably because he was spare and showed bone, and had no belly at all under his belt buckle. But also there was something in his face that opened into unripeness —a tentativeness, an unfinished tone. The hand of an indifferent maker had smeared his mouth and chin and Adam's apple. He was often dealt with as if he were just starting out, heaving his greening masculine forces against life.

The truth was he had been married not once but twice, and both times had lived, a decade all told, in a presentable flat with proper furniture: a crystal chandelier with the first wife, a sleigh-bed with the second, and, with both, scattered low candles in glass balls lit and pulsing at dusk. He had behind him much of the ordinary bourgeois predicament, and had lost it not through intention but through attrition. Neither wife had liked him for long. Birgitta complained that there was something irregular—undigested—in his spirit. Ulrika fought him and stole their daughter from him; he heard from the doleful woman who had been his mother-in-law that they had gone to America. His ex-mother-in-law had no anger for him—she thought him a kind of orphan.

Ulrika's mother was not intelligent, but she was not far wrong. Lars Andemening believed himself to be an arrested soul: someone who has been pushed off a track. He belonged elsewhere. His name was his own fabrication. He had told almost no one—not his wives during all those years, and none of his colleagues at the *Morgontörn*, where he was a once-a-week reviewer—what he understood about himself: that he was the son of a murdered man, a man shot down in the streets over forty years ago, in Poland, while the son was still in the mother's womb. It was a thing he knew and kept buried. There was something dangerous in it, not only because it did not conform—he had been seized in infancy by an unnatural history—but because this father of his was a legend, a dream; or, more exactly, an errant seed thrown back by a corpse. Lars had never learned his mother's name, but his father had become his craze.

His father, a high school art teacher who had lived obscurely in an obscure Galician town, was the author of certain peculiar tales. His name was Bruno Schulz.

For the sake of these tales Lars had saturated himself in Polish, at first on his own, and afterward with an eccentric elderly Polish woman, a retired professor of literature from the University of Cracow; she had escaped to Stockholm with her Jewish husband in the uproar of 1968. Her origins, she said, were high, a family of old blood, used to rigor and noblesse oblige—she would give him his money's worth. She pressed her pupil hard, thrusting Lars from his primer straight into the bosky forests of the between-the-wars modernists. By now Lars was quick enough. He read with a clumsy tongue but a lightning eye, in pursuit of his father's tales.

On account of this father Lars shrank himself. He felt he resembled his father: all the tales were about men shrinking more and more into the phantasmagoria of the mind. One of them was about a man in his sleep, his fall into the bedclothes— like a swimmer against the current; like the captive of a great bowl of dough.

2

IN CASTING OFF his old married ways, Lars had kept nothing but his little daughter's paint set. The telephone on which he had had so many quarrels with Ulrika after she had run off with the child—out! The typewriter that linked him to the literary stewpot—out! He meant to purify his life. Anyone who wanted to get in touch with him had to go through the receptionist at the *Morgontörn*. All these circumstances—these predicaments—gave Lars, God knows how, the face of a foetus; it was as if he was waiting for his dead father to find him, and was determined to remain recognizable.

Yet he was already well into graying. The tall pelt of his head was filigreed with strings the color of goat-milk cheese, and between his entirely beautiful eyes there were two well-established vertical trenches. He was probably on the brink of needing glasses; it was his habit to pull on the cords of his eyebrow muscles, which in turn shot folds across the lids, and these, squeezing down, sharpened his view and deepened the trenches. In spite of such gnarling and graying, he could still be taken, by a stranger on the elevator, for a messenger boy.

On the *Morgontörn* he was one of three reviewers. The others were Gunnar Hemlig, the Wednesday reviewer, and

Anders Fiskyngel, who had Friday. Lars was stuck with Monday: it was settled long ago that no one paid any attention to the culture page on Monday mornings. On buses you could see people yawning their way straight past the headlines to the letters columns, where the anti-alcohol grouches held forth. As the week wore on, the somnolence that characterized the *Morgontörn's* early-edition constituency began to lift. By Wednesday it was ready for Gunnar, an authority on the contemporary American novel; he taught a course on the side, which he called, in the undulations of his recognizable snicker, "The Marriage of Mailer and Jong." By Friday, Anders—who had the favored spot—found the *Morgontörn's* readers alert to any outbreak of temperament. Spy thrillers, royalty, sports, the culinary arts— Anders was insolent in all these categories, and his range of negative specialties was always being augmented. Friday's customers were wide-awake. Nearly a quarter of all the letters the *Morgontörn* received were addressed to Anders Fiskyngel; he was a kind of provocateur, particularly on the subject of flatbread. He was nasty to any cookbook that praised it. It was an instance, he said, of Swedish provincialism.

Few letters came for Lars Andemening. Mondays were worthless. Lars was unread, unmolested, unharassed; he was free. This freedom sent him to bed before evening—not out of indolence. On the wall over his bed he had taped two mottoes:

EVEN LEONARDO DA VINCI HAD ONLY

TWENTY-FOUR HOURS IN A DAY.

******

ARCHIMEDES ALSO SOMETIMES SLEPT.

These were not jokes. Lars, unlike Gunnar, was untouched by the comic muse. He had the chasteness of a consummate gravity. He had long ago thrown himself on the altar of literature. If he slept—secretly—in the afternoon, it was to wring two days out of one.

In the morning he read. This meant that he started on the first page and finished on the last. He was not a skimmer or a sniffer; he read meticulously, as if, swimming, he were being filmed in slow motion. The text swept him away and consumed him—he was like a man (the man in the bedclothes in his father's tale) drawn down by an undertow. Slowly, slowly, the imaginary cinema recorded his heavy resisting gulps. Reading was as exhausting to him as the long, weighted strokes of a drowning man. He gave it all his power. Then he cooked himself a bowl of farina and fell into the wilderness of his quilt.

When he woke at seven into full blackness of night, he felt oddly fat—he was sated with his idea, he understood what he thought. He sat down immediately to his review. He wrote it straight off, a furnace burning fat. It was as if his pen, sputtering along the line of rapid letters it ignited, flung out haloes of hot grease. The air brightened, then charred. He was very quick now, he was encyclopedic, he was in a crisis of inundation. He drove through all the caged hypotheses of his author—some were overt and paced behind bars, others were camouflaged, dappled; he was a dervish, he penetrated everything. When he was within sight of conquest he began to fuzz over with vertigo; he was a little frightened of all he knew. A greased beak tore him off his accustomed ledge and brought him to a high place beyond his control. Something happened in him while he slept. It was not the sleep of refreshment or restoration. He had no dreams. After-ward his lids clicked open like a marionette's and he *saw*: what he saw, before he had formulated even a word of it, was his finished work. He saw it as a kind of vessel, curved, polished, hollowed out. In its cup lay an alabaster egg with a single glittering spot; no, not an egg; a globe, marvelously round. An eye. A human eye: his own; and then not his own. His father's murdered eye.

3

FOR SOME REASON Gunnar Hemlig and Anders
Fiskyngel, enemies of each other—old combatants—both
tolerated Lars. They were not fond of him, but there was little
danger in him and he was rarely underfoot. Unlike Gunnar and
Anders, Lars—possibly because of the ignominy of Monday—
had no cubicle of his own. He appeared at the *Morgontörn*
chiefly to deliver his work and to pick up his messages. He kept
out of most conversations, had no gossip, and seemed, with
regard to office politics, almost newborn. He turned up at ten
o'clock, generally on a Thursday night, to type up his manuscript. Often he would use Anders's typewriter in Anders's
cubicle if Anders was not there; or else Gunnar's. Sometimes
they were both away. But it was not unusual for the two of
them to be smoking or reading, each in his own cubicle, when
Lars arrived, and on these occasions Lars would wander like
an anxious phantom, looking for a desk and a free machine. He
sat wherever there was an empty chair and struggled against
the perversity of the keys. For want of practice he was a bad
typist. He habitually struck a *j* where he intended a *t*, fabricating
strange words.

"North Dakota Swedish," Gunnar said, peering down at Lars's sheet.

"My flat's so cramped," Lars apologized, "it's either keep a typewriter or clean socks."

"Maybe if you typed on your socks, you'd come up with some clean copy," Gunnar said; it was a night when Anders was not there. The place was subject to spectral mutterings—the floorboards had a way of spitting, or growling, or now and then even whistling, under their feet. The *Morgontörn*'s editorial departments were situated in Gamla Stan, the Old Town, around the corner from the Stock Exchange and the Academy, in a neighborhood cleverly rehabilitated for picturesqueness. But the last carpenter to attend to the *Morgontörn*'s forlorn and rickety quarters had lifted his hammer almost eighty years ago; consequently the *Morgontörn* was picturesque only from the street. Inside, it was all ingenious impediment. Its lower façade hinted at the tavern (also named *Morgontörn*, in homage to ancient festivities lasting till dawn) that had occupied that site a hundred and fifty years before. The staff joked that the plumbing had been installed by the tavern's predecessor, an eighteenth-century apothecary who was said to have invented, in a futuristic dream, the water-closet pull chain. The elevator was an inconvenience that could accommodate two persons, on condition that one of them was suitably skeletal.

Lars was thin enough for any purpose. Gunnar remarked that he exactly resembled the building that housed the *Morgontörn*. Gray, narrow, and tall, it had six wretched storeys. The cultural section claimed the topmost floor, where a well-disciplined regiment of mice held their command post. There were heaps of books on every surface. The mice made an orderly meal of them, prefaces for appetizers and indexes for dessert. Skyscrapers of nibbled volumes grew out of the floor and tilted against patched baseboards.

"Minnesota Swedish," Gunnar said. Instead of *tolerans*, Lars had typed *jolerans*; instead of *takt*, *jakt*. "Know what'll help you, Lars? Computerization. Though if it isn't Apple or IBM I don't want it. Leave it to Nilsson, he'll bring them in all Japanese, I'll lay money on it. Not that we'll ever get that far. The electrical system the way it is now can't take it, and Nilsson says he can't get a permit for new wiring until something happens with the walls—God knows what. A collapse maybe."

"I'm happy with my pen," Lars said. He x'd out *jakt* and typed *takt*. He was awkward with machines, but his style was pure. Gunnar's reviews, by contrast, were larded with Americanisms. Gunnar loved everything American, including their fake cheese; on his last trip to New York he had brought back six pounds of Velveeta as a present for his wife.

"Know how long they've been computerized over at *Expressen*?" Gunnar said.

"I'd rather be out here in the Old Town."

"Well, you fit right in," Gunnar said. "Gogol. Balzac—Lucien de Rubempré didn't own a typewriter either. Hooray, there go the walls."

A rumble, a vibration. It was the elevator coming up.

"If that's Anders," Lars said, "I've got to finish this. He'll want his desk."

"He'll want what's *in* it." Gunnar prodded open a drawer. There lay Anders's current bottle, reclining on its side. "You're an exception here, Lars. Not everyone has belles-lettres on the brain day and night. Some have water, and others wine."

The question of Lars and belles-lettres was one of Gunnar's chronic comical points: it frequently signaled a flight of annoyance with Anders. Anders, he maintained, used his choice Friday spot for wheezing and whining; he was out to pull down Swedish self-respect. He was an anti-patriot. The Swedes are a shy people, too modest to bear praise, too withdrawn. But Anders had turned bashfulness inside out; with Anders it was all self-abasement, self-accusation. Self-destruction. It came of being partly

Finnish on his mother's side—you wouldn't expect a sunny disposition in a Finn. "Spits in his own soup," Gunnar persisted.
"In America flatbread is chic, they spread it with caviar. You see
what it comes to. A soiler and a spoiler. When was the last time
he reviewed anything he approved of? When was the last time
he had a good word for something new? Grouses over every writer
since Strindberg. Can't leave anything alone, not even, God
help us, our daily bread."

"*Hej,*" Anders said. His coat was sprinkled with snow rapidly
dissolving into teardrops. "Here's a note for you, Lars. Mrs.
Eklund, who's that? That fool of a girl downstairs, everything
gets stale. I see this is dated last week."

Lars snatched the bit of paper and shoved it into his pocket.
"There's just this last paragraph to do. Two more sentences."

Anders tossed his galoshes into a corner. A startled mouse,
so young it was barely at the cadet stage, jumped out from behind a filing cabinet. "Mrs. Eklund," he repeated. "Start with
taking someone's wife, Lars, no wonder you'll end up taking
someone's desk and chair. Not to mention their vodka." He
stared down at Lars's typing. "You've put *jalteori* for *talteori.*"

"On a Monday," Gunnar said, "who'll notice?"

"My drawer is open," Anders said.

Lars said quickly, "I was looking for an eraser in there—"

"Nobody's touched your vodka," Gunnar said. "Isn't Mrs.
Eklund the one who got you your Polish tutor, Lars?"

"Yet another foreigner," Anders said. "Tell me, is this
Stockholm or Timbuktu?"

"She owns a bookshop," Lars said. "Sometimes I give her
orders."

"I bet you do," Gunnar said.

"Poles and Turks all over town. The deterioration of the
Swedish temperament. The decay of Europe. Litter in downtown
Stockholm. Adultery in bookshops. How about plugging in the
kettle, Lars?"

"I have to go," Lars said.

"Plug in the kettle first, all right? There's nothing like a drop of vodka in a dram of tea to warm up with."

Lars took up Anders's electric kettle and went out into the corridor to the tap just outside the men's toilet. The water, running rusty at the start, barely trickled. He waited for it to clear and then fill. Meanwhile he fished for the message in his pocket: MRS. EKLUND PHONED ABOUT YOUR SISTER. That fool of a girl downstairs. A mistake. He had no sister. When he got back to Anders's cubicle, Anders was rolling up his damp coat on top of the filing cabinet and Gunnar was reading aloud, in a liturgical voice, the first sentence of Lars's typescript: *Here is a universe as confined as a trap, where the sole heroes are victims, where muteness is for the intrepid only.*

"My my," Gunnar said. "What a scare your mother got. I mean when she was pregnant with you. An assault by the higher forms of literature."

"A bad sign," Anders said, "this Polish tutor."

"Leave my papers be," Lars said.

"Mea culpa," Gunnar said, and bowed. "The trouble with you, Lars, is that you're a beautiful soul. A daily reviewer shouldn't be a beautiful soul. It leads to belles-lettres, which leads to exaltation and other forms of decline."

"This pond," Anders said. "This little pond of translators and chameleons. Swedish, the secret language. Who else knows it besides the Swedes? Who else runs to learn everyone else's language? The paralysis of Swedish identity. Pour the water, Lars."

"The Poles are just the same. The Czechs. The Hungarians. We're no worse off than anyone," Gunnar objected. "Why blame the Swedes?"

Lars filled Anders's pink china mug, and Anders measured out a long magnanimous spill of vodka from the bottle in his desk.

"Half the population of Stockholm think they're French philosophers. And the other half"—Anders looked straight at Gunnar—"are circus barkers."

Lars jammed on his stocking cap and picked up his pages. "I'll just leave this on Nilsson's table. Good night, gentlemen."

"A nocturnal visit," Anders asked, "to the Polish tutor?"

"I don't have her any more."

"I'll tell you what your trouble is, Lars. Central Europe, that's your trouble." Gunnar turned his back on Anders, who was allowing the steam from his cup to rise up the two smokestacks of his redoubtable nose, right-angled and attached high at the bridge so as to conceal the other side of his face. "Prague and Vienna and Cracow. A touch of Budapest, a sniff of Bucharest. Throw in Dubrovnik and a handful of Paris misanthropes. You might fetch up Borges from the rump, but otherwise it's all the crazies from the middle. You think my Wednesday people ever heard of this Danilo Kiš? You carry on about him, but they never heard of him. When they move Yugoslavia over to Norway it might be worth a look next door."

"Our Mrs. Eklund," Anders pressed, "can she recommend a tutor in Serbo-Croatian?"

"Don't forget that lemon pulp squeezed out there in the California citrus groves—Adrian Leverkühn, Dr. Faustus! Kafka, Musil, Broch, Canetti, Jabès and Kundera. Those fellows, and don't ignore the ladies, what's her name, Sarraute? The more inscrutable the better. Chasing after the impenetrable. Prince of the indecipherable. *That's* what's eating Monday's brain. What we've got in Lars is a Monday Faust."

Lars finished tying on his scarf. "Gentlemen, I'm off."

The elevator rattled down, swaying on threadbare ropes. All the way to the bottom Lars could hear them clanging away, hammer and tongs. He rarely saw either of them during regular hours; in the clarity of midday he thought them weak, bleached. They were big Viking men, crestfallen. Gunnar had his own kettle in his own cubicle. He kept his things meticulously separate. Thirty years ago he had come to Stockholm from Göteborg; Anders had arrived about the same time from Malmö. They were both night workers who slept the morning away and breakfasted at four in the afternoon. When the daylight foam of ordinariness—secretaries and telephones—cleared out, it pleased them to prowl among the stacks of reviewers' galleys, sniffing after literary prey and flushing out the mice. Even the Niagara of the overhead toilet box in the men's room seemed to them more momentous after midnight. Though they went on contending about this and that—they charged each other with negativism, self-denigration, narrowness—they saw eye to eye on everything; they were privy to what most mattered. They had all the news—which translators cut corners (they agreed that no one could tell the difference between Sven Strömberg's Swedish and Sven Strömberg's Spanish), whose lover had just switched from one critic to another, who was hanging by a hair.

Lars did not know much about their days (they had wives, they had grown children, and Anders even boasted a stepfather of eighty-seven and a still more antediluvian aunt, both imported to Stockholm from Malmö), but he understood their nights. Like himself, they were sunk in books, chained to the alphabet, in thrall to sentences and paragraphs. And beyond this, Lars was charmed by certain corners of their lives. Anders, for instance, had translated, with all its cadences intact, Edgar Allan Poe's "Klockorna"; it was used in a school text and recited by children. Once a month Gunnar crossed the street to have tea with the Librarian of the Academy. He was proud of this, and promised to introduce Lars.

The meeting somehow never materialized, but it was enough for Lars that his own feet took him, almost daily, down the threading alleys of the Old Town and into the open bright square —bright, it struck him, even in rainlight—that skirted the Academy, more sacred to him than any cathedral. He felt his allegiance to all of it: the ten thousand cherished volumes sequestered in those high rooms above the queerly silent Stock Exchange, where computer screens flickered, and a single muffled voice ebbed, and a few old men sat as if in a parliament of statues; the multicolored miles of shelves where the new books, crying the banner of their dust jackets in so many languages, vied for the notice of the Academicians; and, all around, the gray steeples that punctuated the air like pen nibs, up one street and down another. The Library of the Academy was old, old, with old wooden catalogues and long sliding drawers; its records were dispatched by human hands, and had nothing to do with computers. Instead, rows and rows of superannuated encyclopedias were solemnly cradled, like crown jewels, in glass-flanked cabinets in a red-brick cellar. Lars had been to see all this for himself: the benign dungeon, scalloped with monastic arches, and the worktables where specially-appointed scholars set down their burdened briefcases. Those cases: he imagined a plenitude, a robustness, many-stanzaed Eddas, sagas winding on and on. Bliss of scholar-poets, archaeologists of old Norse twilights. The cold gods with their winking breastplates and their hot whims. Hammer of the terrible Thor. Odin and Freya. All diminished into the world's week: the comedy of that.

His father belonged there, in the ventricles of the Academy; Lars was as certain of this as he was of the snow beating against his eyelids. His father had been born to be of that pantheon—with Selma Lagerlöf and Knut Hamsun; with Camus and Pasternak. Shaw, Mann, Pirandello. Faulkner, Yeats, Bellow, Singer, Canetti! Maeterlinck and Tagore. The long, long stupendous list of Winners. His father, if he had lived, would have won the great Prize—it was self-evident. He was of that magisterial company.

4

THERE WAS a bitter wind now, lording it over the black of one o'clock. The blackness went on throwing the snow into Lars's face, and he packed his scarf over his nose and mouth—how warm his breath was in the little cave this made! He hurried past the Stock Exchange and the Academy—not a lit bulb anywhere, or even the daub of a watchman's flashlight. Succession of whitening roofs: how easy to see into the thickest dark through a lens of snow. The spiraling flakes stuttered around him like Morse code. A smell of something roasting, what was that? Chimneys. It was clear to him finally that he was walking fast and far; tramping, trotting; he had already traversed the bridge over the locks, where the salty Baltic fought the rush of fresh waters to the death; he caught where he was heading. That burning. He listened for fire engines. O the chimneys. Quiet everywhere: here was the street where Nellie Sachs and her old mother had once lived. The poet's flat; the poet's windows. All moribund there. He came to the end of Bergsundsstrand at a boiling pace, overheated under his scarf and cap. The few cars with their sleepless headlights slipped by like slow cats. Stockholm, an orderly city, has its underlife, its hidden wakeful. Whoever owns a secret in Stockholm turns and turns in the night emptiness, but not in sleep.

Under the screen of revolving flakes the steeples had the look of whirling Merlin hats. Twenty streets behind him, the voices of Gunnar and Anders, beating, flying. Gull cries. Even now, when he was not there. Rodomontade, long-winded rococo affectations, what poseurs! Shelfworn, shopworn, scarred and marred. It was mainly their scratches that took Lars's love, their weakness, their comedown. They were like Tiu, Odin's son, god of war, god of victory. First Fanrir the wolf bites off one whole hand. Then all the rest of powerful Tiu—head, torso, and three strong remaining limbs—is reduced to being only Tuesday. Also, Lars loved their maimed scribblers' odor, pale and dimly prurient, a fuminess skimmed from the *Morgontörn*'s omnipresent staleness, like some fungus regenerated out of antiquity. For all Lars knew, he too was infiltrated by this smell. The mice were innocent. Their militarily clean pellets left no scent.

That roasting in the air. His own sweat. The exertion. His legs like gyros. O the chimneys of armpits, moist and burning under wool. Ahead, he made out the mullioned door of Heidi's shop. She was often among the nighttime wakeful. A woman of sixty-five or so, a round little bundle, with a girl's name. She wore curly bangs, like a girl; but they were white and sheeplike, and dropped in ringlets over two serenely misplaced black mustaches that jumped intermittently above reckless eyes. Reckless and cherry-dark, with toughened skins for lids. Saccharine, to call a child after a figment in a novel. The Germans are sentimental. Their word *Heimweh*. The English say homesick; the same in plain Swedish. *Hemsjuk*. Leave it to the Germans to pull out, like some endless elastic belt of horrible sweetness, all that molasses woe. Heidi, in self-appointed exile, denied any twinge of *Heimweh*; she spat on it. She was practical and impatient, and had long ago given up ridiculing her name. In the last decades, she explained, it had, in fact, begun to suit her. It

was as if by the principle of her own obstinacies she had changed
its disposition: from tremulous edelweiss to the forces of a determined old strictness. Lars was not extremely afraid of her; but
he was a little afraid.

In the skimpy vestibule of her shop he stamped his boots so
hard they splashed up icy rods from their treads. He saw the light
in the narrow back room, a sort of corridor behind the high rear
bank of bookshelves, and supposed she was totting up her in-
voices, or else unpacking the week's shipment. She was unusually
strong for such a small rotundity, such a thick globular dwarf of
a woman, and could heave those dead-weight overseas boxes on
her own; though when the shop was open she kept a Turkish
boy to lug things. Or, he reflected, she might be sitting under
her funny old lamp (the lamp, she said, was all she thought
worth bringing with her from Germany, not counting a handful
of books), reading whatever had just arrived—she read her wares,
in nearly any language. Her wares were international. They
glimmered out at him from the display window: shining rec-
tangles, like portraits in frames—the newest Americans, North
and South, the oldest Russians, that large and steady company
of nineteenth-century Englishmen and Englishwomen, a modi-
cum of Czechs and Poles, a whole forest of Balzac; and then the
dictionaries and encyclopedias. The shopwindow was stuffed
from floor to ceiling: a step-pyramid crowded, on each level, with
all the alphabets. Erect in the middle of it, like the thrusting
central rose in a wreath, or like a sentry guarding a vault, stood—
it really did stand, as if on lion's legs—a formidable edition of
Drottningholm: ett kungligehem, with color pictures of the Royal
Family: the wavy-haired King tall and fair and unperturbed, the
two little Princesses charming in a garden, the diffident little
Prince in a sailor suit on a damask sofa, and the shiveringly beautiful Queen, with her brilliant teeth and black Iberian eyes. The
Queen was said to be brainy, a descendant of Marrano nobility.
Secret Jews, long attenuated. Heidi was now a Swedish patriot.

When the Royal Family was sold out, she displayed one of those oversized landscape volumes, itself as extensive as a plain, showing photographs of windmills and castles and deer galloping over snow and the sea gulls of Lake Vänern and a statue of Selma Lagerlöf, seated, with her hair in a bronze bun.

Lars took out his penknife and tapped on the glass door. No one heard. He tapped again. She might have left the light on and gone home to her flat. Lars had made her his confidante— Heidi was one of those few who knew what he knew—and still he had never been to her flat. Her flat was no more a certainty than any other rumor; no more a certainty than the rumor of her husband, Dr. Eklund. The true signature of her matrimonial relation appeared in gold letters painted across the shopwindow: BOKHANDLARE. When she turned the key in the evening she embraced her two-burner stove and her square small table and her cot. Among the bumpy configurations of cartons in the back room she had a tiny refrigerator and a tiny water closet and a blue-speckled porcelain pot and that funny old German lamp— the shade was a crystal daffodil—and a teakettle. She had no bath at all, though there was a secluded hollow, a sort of alley, that might have closeted a shower. And no radio: nothing for music. She was indifferent to music. It was as if she were a forest gnome who had fashioned a bare little hut for herself, with only one ornament: the necessary daffodil.

The light wavered, dimmed, returned. A figure had passed in front of it. Once again Lars smacked his penknife against the glass. And there was Heidi with her blurred German screech— "All right, all right, the world isn't coming to an end, you'll crack my door!"—wheeling across her shop to let him in.

Lars resumed stamping his boots in the vestibule. "*Hej,*" he said.

"Well, get them *off*. I won't have you drip those things in here. For heaven's sake, the floor's been mopped. Just leave them. You always show up at my busiest time."

"You're closed up tight!" But he was used to absurdities in her. She liked to topple him.

"When else do you think I can get anything done? Not with customers underfoot all day. I'm sorting out a delivery. I'm trying to price things. My God, I'm *concentrating*. And now you'll want coffee."

"No," he said, standing on the doorsill in his stocking feet. "*Sprit.*"

"No wonder. You're a stick of ice. A snowman."

"I'm boiling hot," he contradicted, and followed her into the back room. "I stink of sweat." He was not in the least meek with her. He was meek with Gunnar and Anders because they deserved it; they were insufficient. But with Heidi he could be coarse. It hid his small fear.

"That you do. You smell like a rutting sheep. I've got your order—all these Slavs. Don't expect them to come cheap. They weren't easy to get hold of, believe me. Two are in English, from the States. I couldn't find them any other way." A long yawn, sumptuous, leisurely, disclosed the gold in her molars. A sleep-crease marked her left cheek. Pillow and blanket were in disorder on her cot. She hauled a canvas bag off a shelf behind the German lamp and drew out a pair of paperbacks. "Ludvík Vaculík, there. Bohumil Hrabel, there. Witold Gombrowicz, I've got him right here. Nobody but you wants such stuff."

"There was supposed to be another—"

"The other Polish one. Where did I put . . . here. Tadeusz Konwicki, here he is. Hardcover. Him I could track down only in Polish. Your native language," she said with a lift of her sardonic little shoulder.

She handed him a tiny glass of vodka and yawned again. Stingy. He saw she was going to stay annoyed with him. She knew what he knew; she knew it all, every permutation of every speculation; they had talked and talked about what he knew until it was all ground down into granules. His history—

his passion—was no more than a pile of salt between them. There was no longer anything left for them to sift through. She had, besides, a hard skepticism for every grain of it—even for his Polish, though she had herself introduced him to his teacher, one of her own customers. It was the cast of her mind to run from self-irony to blatancy—insofar as Lars could guess anything at all about what her mind was like. Her Swedish was cocky and pliant, but it had the whole tune of German, and when she let out into it, as she frequently did, a German syllable or two, it seemed to Lars that he could, for just that instant, look down through a trapdoor into a private underground chamber where no one was allowed to follow. For all her noisiness, she was bitingly private. Her husband, for instance—the mysterious, the distant, the vaporous Dr. Eklund—was either a psychoanalyst or a gastroenterologist: she hinted sometimes at one, sometimes at the other. And her life before—what was that? She wanted not to be what she had been before. She had arrived in Stockholm after the war, like so many others. She had been quick to marry Dr. Eklund.

Between Heidi's back room and the public space of the shop a fence of books reared up. Now and then Lars imagined that Dr. Eklund was hiding out there on the other side, beyond the reach of the daffodil's yellow arc. Or he imagined that Dr. Eklund was dead. Cremated. His remains were in the big coffee tin on the shelf behind the lamp; Heidi was a widow. It occurred to Lars that he would like to marry such a woman, independent, ungenial, private, old; a kind of heroine.

He was glad she was old. It meant she was prepared to be proprietary—the old have a way of taking over the young. She regarded Lars as her discovery—a discovery four years in the past that, she said, she had grown to regret. She had stumbled on him kneeling next to his briefcase among the S's in FOREIGN FICTION—a new face in the shop, and already he was dawdling there, for an hour or more, over a copy of *Cinnamon Shops* in

Polish. She clapped her hands at him, the way you clap your hands to shoo away a harmless animal, and he circled slowly round to absorb her anger, not startled, but oddly distracted, like someone who has had a vision: it came to him instantly that he would tell this old woman what he knew about himself. The shape of her head drew him—small, jumbled, those curly bangs white as a sheep fallen over the wobbly mustaches. He had never seen such eyebrows. Her head was a sheep's head, but she was as shrewd and impatient as a lion. She warned him that she wouldn't allow her merchandise to look shopworn before sale; he was in plenty of trouble with her—she had been watching him turn the pages over; a hundred times. It was true. He had washed his fingers in that half-familiar dread print like a butcher with a bloody sheep in his grip, or like a tug dragging a river for a body.

"My father wrote this," he told her.

She seized the book from his hands and slipped it back into its slot on the shelf of foreign S's.

"It's five o'clock," she said. "We're closing now."

"I would buy it," Lars said, "but I can't really read it yet."

"Then go home and learn Polish."

"I'm doing that," he said, and pulled his Polish grammar out of his briefcase to show her.

"You bought that somewhere else. We don't carry that, it's not the best one."

"I'm a refugee. I was born in Poland." He shoved away his grammar and reached down again for *Cinnamon Shops*. "My native language, and I can't read it."

"If you're not going to purchase that book," she said sharply, "put it back."

"It's already mine," he said, "by inheritance."

"Put it back, please. We're closing now."

He was afraid she would push him out the door. Her voice was oily, elongated, ironic: she thought him a crazy man. He stood his ground; he had chosen her, he had made up his mind. She was the one. He explained how, newborn, pulled from the fork of his mother, he was smuggled, through all the chaos over the face of the deep that was the logic of that time, to a relative in Stockholm—a poor scared refugee herself, an elderly cousin with a sliver of luck. A handful of other infants had been spirited away from Poland—Poland overrun by Nazis—and squeezed into Stockholm under the same auspices: a merciful Swedish traveler, well-paid, under the protection of her government's neutrality. Like any story that hangs on suffering, chance, whim, stupidity in the right quarters, mercy and money, there was something random to it—a randomness that swelled and swelled like an abscess. The elderly cousin, lost in bewilderment, fell away, and Lars, while the war went on, found himself in the household of the widowed sister-in-law of the merciful mercenary traveler's own cousin. This sister-in-law already had a son, and did not need another; she took Lars anyhow, despite his brown eyes, and thanked her stars as he grew that he could be mistaken —as long as no one suspected anything different—for Swedish. She did not like the looks of other nations, especially those more distant from the Arctic Circle than her own. Lars ripened into ingratitude, and at sixteen left home to live alone in someone's attic room. He met his rent by getting a job as a messenger boy on a newspaper. Already he knew his future was print.

All this Heidi listened to in a concentration of rage. He was just then describing how he had invented a new surname for himself straight out of the dictionary—she stopped him right there in the middle. She shut the lights, locked the door, and drew him with her into her back room; she sat him down under the crystal daffodil and spat her dry gargle into her tiny sink. "Why do you tell me these things? Why should I want to know? You think you're the only one with a story? Stockholm is full of refugees! All my customers are refugees! Professors! Intellectuals! I have my own story!"

Lars curved his thumb into the darkened shop. "You've got my father out there. In the original. This is the only place in Stockholm that has him in the original."

"Your father! There's something wrong with you, you're a *Verrückter*, how can you say who your father is with a story like that!"

He gave this some thought. "Well, in a way you're right—I don't know who my mother is. I've never found out."

"You don't know your father either!"

"No, no, you can see the resemblance. All those photos—"

"What photos, where? Where did you get them, who gave them to you?"

"Photos in books, I mean."

"Oh, books! If they don't come from family—"

"I've got every detail of his face, I know it by heart. I know almost every word he ever wrote. Father and son. We look alike, two peas in a pod. It's the same nose, you see how my chin comes to a point? And it isn't even a matter of looks. There's an affinity. His voice. His mind."

A great hornlike snort burst from her. But she was letting him have his say; she wasn't throwing him out. He watched her dip a big spoon into the tin on the shelf behind the lamp—right into what might have been Dr. Eklund's ashes. She was brewing him some coffee. "Theatrical. Self-pity. You're an orphan? An orphan is alive, what's the matter with that? Besides, you're a Swede like any Swede. Why be a fool and dredge all that up— nobody cares, old Nazi stories, you think anyone cares any more?"

"They shot him in the streets. Murdered. The underground got him false papers—in those times forgery was a sacrament. They had already found him a hiding place. But he wouldn't leave home. He was glued there."

"And where did you learn all this? Also from books?"

"I've read everything. There's nothing I haven't read. I've read *Cinnamon Shops* a thousand times over. I can't tell you how many times I've read the other one. But in translation. It's my father, I need to read the original—"

"The original!"

"The Polish."

"The Polish, yes." She splashed a full cup down before him. "A stranger, a lunatic probably, comes into my shop, mangles the merchandise, doesn't buy a thing, claims he's a Pole, can't read a word of Polish, and here I am serving him coffee! God knows what my husband would make of this. Dr. Eklund," she said, "takes an interest in original behavior. Dr. Eklund and I understand exactly what you are."

"I've announced what I am."

"An impostor. Another refugee impostor. It's nothing new, believe me! Half my customers have made themselves up. Fabricators. Every Pole of a certain age who walks in here, male or female, used to be a famous professor in Warsaw. Every Hungarian was once ambassador to Argentina. The French are the worst. I've never had one of those in my shop who didn't turn out to be just the one who got Sartre started on the Talmud. By now I've counted twenty-five female teachers of Talmud— poor Mlle. de Beauvoir."

"It's a Polish teacher *I* want," Lars said.

"Done. I'll get you the fanciest professor I can think of. There's a lady from Cracow, extremely literary, in fact a member of the nobility, a Radziwill actually, related to the husband of the sister of the American Onassis—she used to own a hat store. She gives Polish lessons. Her husband was just as good a Communist as the ones who chased him out. You'll have to play along and call her Doctor, unless she makes you call her Princess. Her father was a *maître d'*. Her mother was a milliner."

He saw then that what he had taken for rage was something else: a fever of isolation. She was often alone, especially after hours—Dr. Eklund, she said, had his late rounds at the hospital; sometimes he had to go out of town. But the shop was quiet even in the middle of the day. An afternoon might pass without a single customer. Lars observed that the crammed window display seldom changed. The only books in the window that shook off their dust were the Royal Family and the photographs of northern landscapes. The tourists bought these, Americans and English and Germans. There was not so much demand for foreign books—you could find practically anything in translation. As for the refugees, they had all learned Swedish long ago. The Academy was always ordering foreign books, of course, but it got them directly from abroad; it wouldn't bother with a little local bookshop, would it? And off the beaten path, who even knew it was there? Despite these troubles, Heidi said, she managed to make ends meet, but if it weren't for Dr. Eklund's encouragement—not to mention his tiding her over now and then—where would she be? The shop ran—well, not on faith, she didn't believe in the invisible, but on something else just as unreliable: it ran on human oddity. You never could tell what kind of human curiosity might walk in and spend two thousand kroner. Dr. Eklund was a great collector of such curiosities. Tangled lives appealed to him. From his patients he picked up the most bizarre histories. A bookshop is the same—a magnet for freaks, gypsies, nomads. Last month a genuine sheikh had turned up, burnoose and all, in sandals, stockingless, his toenails painted red and matted over with snow, looking for the *Kama Sutra* in Arabic.

"And did you have it?" Lars asked.

"We were just out. It's one of my biggest sellers."

It seemed to Lars finally that Heidi had not only not intended to throw him out—she had more or less kidnapped him and locked him in with her. It was difficult to gauge, since then, who was whose captive. Lars came and went whenever he pleased, though he could never be sure of a welcome. "Ha, it's you," Heidi would say, scowling. "Just when I'm expecting Dr. Eklund. He should be here any minute now." A ruin of gloomy

creases traveled through the black mustaches. "It's your footsteps—they sound exactly like Dr. Eklund's. Light as smoke."
This meant Dr. Eklund was again delayed, or else had gone
straight home to the flat. Another time she blamed the Turkish
boy for writing up an order for Lars. "Mr. Andemening doesn't
really *want* it. He's not a customer. Nothing from him goes into
the order book unless *I* put it there, do you understand? In his
business he gets all the books he wants for free, and if he orders
something here, it's only because he likes to make a show of earn-
ing his keep." Once she presented Lars with a volume thick as a
brick—it was the other Polish grammar, the really good one he
didn't own. But mostly the traffic between them went the other
way: every two weeks or so Lars thudded down right there on
Heidi's cash-register counter a load of discarded reviewers' copies
from the *Morgontörn*. This excited her always. She was interested to know whether Anders had reviewed any of these, and
which ones Gunnar had cast off. She read these gentlemen in
the *Morgontörn* on Wednesdays and Fridays; she liked Fridays
better, because Mr. Fiskyngel was so cantankerous; it was amusing. Mr. Hemlig often *tried* to be amusing, and that was less
amusing. She rarely said a word to Lars about Mondays, and
if she did, it was again to topple him: "*Furchtbar!* Ordinary
people have no patience for that sort of thing. After all, a newspaper isn't a university seminar. I'm surprised they keep you on.
—Good God, that devilish little Turk's got your name down in
the order book again. After I've told him and told him not to
go scribbling—"

Lars broke in: "An assignment from the Princess."

"If it's Polish books you want, you should come straight to
me. How can a little Turk—"

"You were out. He said you'd gone to get groceries."

"Groceries! Wasn't that Wednesday? In the late afternoon?
I went with Dr. Eklund to buy a new suit. He likes me there to
select the fabric. He won't choose even a necktie if I'm not with

him." She squinted down at Lars's order through the big magnifiers of her reading glasses. "*Sanatorium pod Klepsydra.* It's a miracle that boy got it down right. We don't keep it in stock anyhow, you can see for yourself it's only *Cinnamon Shops* on the shelf."

"This is the one he wrote after *Cinnamon Shops.* The second one. The one before the last—*The Messiah* was the last."

"Well, I can guarantee you my jobber won't have it."

"Your jobber," Lars burst out, "won't have *The Messiah,* no! No one has it. It's lost."

"These things have to come from Warsaw," Heidi said placidly, "lost or found. It may take weeks."

"Too long. The Princess won't like it, she'll be annoyed. She can't wait for the finish. She's getting ready to throw me out. I'm practically dismissed. On my own. Kicked out."

"You'd think she'd want to hang on to you. For the money at least."

"First she says I'm coming along at a tremendous rate, and the next minute she wants to get rid of me. She doesn't believe in me, that's why."

Heidi snorted, "Believe in you! What are you, a priest, a holy man?"

"She won't accept it."

"Accept what, for God's sake?"

"That I'm my father's son."

"You shouldn't have talked about that. A craziness to talk about that! And you say you keep it to yourself, you never talk about it at all, you never tell it, *I'm* the only one—"

"You are."

"Oh, yes! Myself, and Mrs. Rozanowska, and Mr. Fiskyngel, and Mr. Hemlig—"

"I've never told anyone at the paper."

"A woman gives you Polish lessons, you tell *her.*"

"An accident. I didn't intend to. She was making me read

out loud to her. She's been trying to fix my accent. So I picked out the part about furniture—you know, furniture breaking out in a rash. My father's own syllables—there they were, coming out of my mouth. In my own voice. In the original."

"Poor Mrs. Rozanowska. She's afraid you're deranged."

"*She* thinks she's a Princess!"

"She doesn't *think* so. She only says so."

5

AFTER THAT Lars felt a change: a thickening between them. She was all at once willing to be entangled with him. She began to question him about how he lived—he was clearly fond of looking alert in the middle of the night. Lars hesitated to tell her how out of the power of his secret dreamless sleep he had learned to enter his father's throat; to see his father's eye. The terrifying germ and nucleus of his origin. In the end he told her he slept in daylight. The rest he kept to himself; there was sorcery in it. Otherwise he withheld nothing from her. He was not certain whether *she* believed he was his father's son—she acknowledged that she believed he believed it. He came almost every night now. She cooked him dinner in the back room— while Dr. Eklund was away it was more convenient to live in the shop, she explained, than in the flat: Dr. Eklund was attending a mental health conference in Copenhagen. It would last more than a week, and since Dr. Eklund was giving a paper in the final seminar, he was obliged to stay to the bitter end. For dinner she mainly scrambled eggs mixed with onion. Lars peeled and chopped the onions on a board on the tiny table. He wept drearily. It was the fumes that set him off, but the tears derived from reasons of the heart. He was grateful: Heidi had fallen into his condition alongside him, a companion, a fellow collector of his father's fate, a kind of partner. She was already intimate with his father's books—no great feat, she said, since the man's whole canon, after all, consisted of two lone volumes.

"Three," Lars said. "Don't forget *The Messiah*."

"Not if it's lost. It doesn't exist. You can't count what doesn't exist."

"But if we're speaking of everything he wrote—"

"It doesn't matter what he wrote. The only thing that matters is what's here to be read."

"The manuscript might have survived somehow. Nobody knows what happened to it."

"If it disappeared it was destroyed."

"Or else it wasn't destroyed. It might be hidden. When the Nazis came he gave it away for safekeeping."

"And even if he did give it away it evaporated. It doesn't exist," Heidi said again. "Whoever had it was hauled off. You're always expecting what isn't there to *be* there." She opened out derisive palms: small callused squares that had, by now, a familiar way of accusing him. She thought him a master of the insubstantial: a fantasist. Often enough she threw out at him her special taunt: "*Hauch*," she liked to say—his ideas were no more than a breath of air; she did not regard them.

It was the shooting that drew her. The shooting; the murder. Shot in the streets! Lars suspected that Heidi cared more for his father's death than for his father's tales, where savagely crafty nouns and verbs were set on a crooked road to take on engorgements and transmogrifications: a bicycle ascends into the zodiac, rooms in houses are misplaced, wallpaper hisses, the calendar acquires a thirteenth month. Losses, metamorphoses, degradations. In one of the stories the father turns into a pincered crab; the mother boils it and serves it to the family on a dish. Heidi shouldered all that aside: it was the catastrophe of fact she wanted, Lars's father gunned down in the gutters of Drohobycz along with two hundred and thirty other Jews. A Thursday in 1942, as it happened: the nineteenth of November. Lars's father was bringing home a loaf of bread.

They settled in to their night's work: the recitation of scraps. By now they had gathered up every shred and grain; still, their stock was small. Heidi had discovered on her own shelves—misplaced behind Tuwim the poet—Lars's father's translation of Kafka's *The Trial*. Lars was less pleased with this than she had expected. He complained that he didn't care for his father in the role of the dummy on Franz Kafka's lap; it was his father's own voice he was after. But when Heidi somehow finagled from a dealer she was acquainted with a brittle browning copy of the Warsaw weekly in which "The Comet" had first appeared, Lars felt an onion-sting of joy. His nose moistened. It was like coming on a missing pair of gloves—how it warmed his hands! The look of Polish had begun finally to fit his eyesockets without estrangement, and it was the weight in his heated hands of that dog-eared rust-speckled journal, dated fifty years back, that made him forgive the Princess for casting him out. He didn't need her; he was on his own. He read—he could read!—how the father in "The Comet" thrusts a microscope into a chimney shaft and examines the starlight that has infiltrated into the sooty darkness: the star is composed of a human brain with an embryo sunk inside. Heidi was indifferent to the notion of a homunculus in the sky. She told Lars it was all madness. Images in magnetic batches. She scolded him for turning his father into some sort of ceremonial mystification; there was a smoldering cultishness in all of it. His father's tales—animism, sacrifice, mortification, repugnance! Everything abnormal, everything wild.

Still, Heidi stuck by him; she wasn't throwing him out, like the Princess. Heidi appeared to be as absorbed in their little stock as he was: together they combed through the letters, one by one, taking turns reading them out. With their heads close they gazed into the photographs. Lars's young father was always the central figure, the only male, ringed round by women. Lars memorized each woman's face. One of these might easily be the face of his father's lover—any one of them. Any one of them might be Lars's own mother. Heidi disagreed: Lars's father— they knew this from the letters—was too withdrawn, too isolated, too obsessive, to have gone casually into a woman's bed. And the women themselves: these faces: they were too worldly, too lightly content, too *exterior*, to belong to someone who might become Lars's father's lover. His lover must be elsewhere, in a secret place beyond the photos. She would need to be a poet. There were so many letters written to literary women. Romana Halpern? No. Zofia Nalkowska? No. Deborah Vogel? No. All these candidates were, for this and that good reason, wrong. Besides, there was the fact of Jozefina: the Catholic fiancée, still alive. An old woman. Well into her eighties, perhaps, living in London.

"You should go over there," Heidi said, "and find out her side of the story. Before it's too late."

"What do I need London for? We *know* her side. She wanted to settle in Warsaw after the wedding. She even spoke of Paris. And *he* wouldn't budge out of Drohobycz. Stuck. Paralyzed."

"She's a living witness to the man. She could tell you things. She could tell you why the wedding didn't come off. You should talk to her."

Lars said grimly, "She was his enemy."

"She loved him more than he loved her—he said so himself! As if we didn't read *exactly* that letter less than a week ago! As if I hadn't broken my head getting *hold* of that letter!"

"She wanted him to be normal," Lars said.

They went back and forth in this way, on every point, piecing things out, quarreling. Tracings, leavings, enigmatic vestiges—over each tendril they had their calculations and speculations and probings and puzzlings. Drohobycz itself a puzzle: a place recorded on the map of Poland only in the tiniest print. It was hardly there at all. To push through into the scenery and substance of Drohobycz was like entering a pinhole. The hasidim of the neighborhood—gone. Lars's father's father's shop —a drygoods business—gone. Nothing left; not a ribbon, not a thimble. Between Drohobycz and Lars's father there had occurred a mutual digestion. Street by street, house by house, shop by shop, Lars's father had swallowed Drohobycz whole; Drohobycz was now inside every tale. And Drohobycz had swallowed Lars's father also: a drab salary, a job he despised, a band of relatives to support—paralyzed, stuck, how was it possible to leave? Lars's father was a gargoyle on the flank of Drohobycz, a mole on its inmost sinew. Once he traveled to Warsaw. Once he traveled to Lvov. Once he even went as far as Paris! But in the end he came home to be digested. All those weighty names Heidi recited out of the letters, poets and painters and philosophers and novelists, sometimes two or three in the same person—Stanislaus Witkiewicz, for instance, famously nicknamed Witkacy—what kind of living ghost did they think they were addressing, a high school teacher of arts and crafts, smeared with provincial paste and paint? Underground, immobile, cut off. Jozefina wanted him baptized after their engagement. He refused, but offered a concession: he would forsake the world of the Jews. His family had anyhow always kept their distance from the teeming outlandish hasidim in their long black coats. He was a Pole: he had already thrown himself on the unyielding breast of mother Poland, and nestled into the underside of her tongue. If he had ever sipped a word or two of Yiddish out of the air, it did not ride his spittle or his pen.

These were their accumulations and incidentals. They understood how little they had. They folded and unfolded the layers of Lars's father's thin life—it grew thinner yet. They had scratched out of Drohobycz all there was to scratch, and out of the poor fiancée the same. They were, they saw, nearly finished—

it was squeezing milk from a stone to hope for more. The rest
was quotations, excerpts, recitations. Vyings. Heidi had traced
down a handwritten memoir: an account of a dinner party at
which Lars's father and his fiancée are guests. Lars's father
eats without emitting a syllable, mute; meanwhile the elegant
Jozefina is animated, talkative. The bride chirps, the bride-
groom is dumb. The memoirist thinks to herself: *There will be
no bread from this flour*. An old proverb, and prophetic: no marriage followed. And one night Lars telephoned from the *Morgontörn* to announce the recovery, from Anders's trash basket, of
an American review. An American review! An amazement. Both
books are reviewed. In America they call *Cinnamon Shops* by
another name: *The Street of Crocodiles*, after one of the most
horrifying of the tales. The second book is called in English
Sanatorium Under the Sign of the Hourglass—an endless train
of hissings. The lost third one isn't mentioned. "He's reached
across finally," Lars said, agitated, "he's passed beyond little
Europe." He promised to bring the review to Heidi's shop within
the hour, to lay it, so to speak, at her feet. It seemed to him that
hers was the only brain in Stockholm able to value such an
offering. But when he arrived the black mustaches were wobbling: she was all victory and spite. She flashed at him an out-of-
the-way periodical.

"Look what's here! A letter! A new one. Published for the
first time." There was an engine in her breathing; she was
pumping out elation. "He's writing in 1934. Eight years before
the shooting. Listen to this! *I need a companion. I need a
kindred spirit close by me. I long for an acknowledgment of the
inner world whose existence I postulate.* And you think you can
come in here bragging about finding an American review! What's
a review? Nothing. Listen! *I would like to lay my burden on
someone else's shoulder for a moment. I need a partner in
discovery*—"

Lars said hoarsely, "Where did you get all that?"

"I keep my eye out. I have my sources. If there's something that hasn't come home to roost, leave it to me to dig it up."

"He means me," Lars said. "I'm the one he means."

"Please. So much and no farther. This is years before you were born."

"You don't understand him. You don't know. He's thinking of the future. A laying-on of hands. He's thinking ahead."

"He's thinking of a woman," Heidi said. "It's a woman he wants. *A partner in discovery*—that's a wife, isn't it?"

"A son. *An acknowledgment of the inner world*—it can't be a wife. He keeps his privacy, it's not a wife he wants. He never *had* a wife. He can give up Jozefina, but not solitude. Solitude is just the thing he won't give up. The burden is sent ahead—a signal through the genes. The partner in discovery is the next generation."

Heidi struck off a click of exasperation. "If he isn't looking for a woman, why else are there all those letters to women?"

"Ha!" Lars said; he felt the advantage shift. He could out-think her; he would make her pay for belittling the American review. "The life of a recluse—nobody comes in or out of the house, except through letters. He lives on correspondence. People leave him alone. The mitigation of solitude without the bother of human flesh."

"Your mother," Heidi tossed back, "wasn't a piece of paper."

"My father turned everything into paper." He took in a brief preparatory pinch of air. "*Reality is as thin as paper*—"

"Don't spout that again. I know what it's going to be. It's what you always—"

"*Reality is as thin as paper and betrays with all its cracks* . . ."

". . . *its intuitive character*," Heidi finished. "Nincompoopery. Standing things on their head. What's real is real."

She fell back into her chair under the daffodil; she had the sleepy look he often thought to be secretive. He was conscious once again of having bested her. It had become a contest between them—a contest of assimilation and disclosure. She had, for a while, pulled up equal with him, shoulder to shoulder; she was right there beside him. She comprehended, she engulfed, she devoured. She *had* things—she had facts, she had everything *he* had; she knew and kept it all. And in the end she was no more than an onlooker. It wasn't fair: even when she pulled up equal she wasn't equal; she could never be equal, because the author of *Cinnamon Shops*, the author of *Sanatorium*, the author of the vanished *Messiah*, wasn't her father. Lars had to be, in the nature of it, ahead—always, always; he was his father's son.

She punished him for it by orphaning him; again and again she led him back to the shooting. She came to it by a dozen routes. Each time it was a surprise, an ambush. She could begin anywhere, and still she would smash Lars into Thursday, that Thursday, the Thursday of the shooting: Thursday the nineteenth of November. They discovered—Heidi's research—that the terrible day had a name among the Jews of Drohobycz: Black Thursday. And the hunt itself, the hunt for Jews in the streets, was called "the wild action." No matter how wary Lars tried to be, Heidi was canny enough to catch him up in the wild action. Her snares were ingenious. Had Lars been mooning once more over the missing *Messiah*? It ended in the wild action; in a camp; in murder. It was known that Lars's father had handed over the manuscript—to whom? when?—for its preservation. What had become of *The Messiah* and its keeper? Was its keeper man or woman, neighbor or stranger? Killed in the wild action, on Black Thursday? Or else deported, gassed. The corpse thrown into the oven; smoke up the chimney. And *The Messiah*? If its keeper was shot in the street, was *The Messiah* scattered loose in the gutter, to be chewed over by dogs, to rot in the urine of cats? Or was *The Messiah* shut up in an old dresser in a house in Drohobycz until this day? Or put out with the trash thirty-five years ago? Or left tangled between its

keeper's coat and shoes in the mountain of coats and shoes behind a fence in the place of death?

Whatever they touched on, Heidi rattled her links—everything belonged to the shooting. Everything was connected to the
shooting. Were they leafing through Lars's father's drawings?
They were sure to run into the wild action; the wild action was
irresistible. The drawings were unearthly enough on their own—
dwarfish, askew, psychological, symbolical. Abnormal. The drawings, what were they? Frozen panic. Wildness transfixed. Lars's
father himself, in a letter to Witkacy, spoke of them as predestined images, *ready and waiting for us at the very beginning
of life.* There was one of a top-hatted gentleman who has just
walked out of an arbor into town; an importuning thick-necked
beast in a business suit—a dog of some kind—is resting a heavy
paw on the gentleman's elbow, urging, entreating. Some distance
off, hidden among trees, a man stands watching, his whole head
swallowed by leafiness. This picture had attracted the taste of a
certain Gestapo officer. On account of the drawings he undertook
to become the artist's "protector." The Gestapo officer gave Lars's
father a special pass out of the ghetto—they had set up a little
ghetto in Drohobycz—to the Aryan side of town. There was
bread on that side, so off Lars's father went. It was the day of the
wild action, the S.S. out suddenly in swarms; even so, Lars's
father was not shot randomly. An S.S. man recognized him as
the Gestapo officer's Jew and gunned him down. The S.S. man
was said to be the Gestapo officer's "rival." Rival in what? Rival
for what?

"You make everything come out in the same place," Lars
complained. "The wrong place. That's not how it's supposed to
go. You get me off the track. You make me lose the thread."

"The thread? The thread? What's this thread? What's this
track?"

"My father's books. His sentences."

"Nouns and verbs! You think that's what it's about, nouns and verbs? *Sentences!* Subjects! Predicates! Pieces of paper!"

"Language. Literature. My father's"—he let out a sigh no wider than a filament—"genius."

"Go knock at the door of the Academy and tell them to let your father in."

"They'd have given him the Prize if he'd lived."

"Well, maybe there's still a chance. Maybe they'll change the rules and start giving it to skeletons."

A shock: she could see straight through to the skeleton. Without warning he understood how it was that Heidi could make him afraid. Skeletons. Everyone who walked by her. All her refugee customers. Probably even that Turkish boy—she abused him, she barked at him. Not to mention Lars's ex-tutor, the phony Princess, who was plump enough. And what of Dr. Eklund? Dr. Eklund, turning beside her in bed in the rushings of the night— the big connubial bed of their flat—did she drill clear through to the xylophone of the ribs? And the tall infantile graying head of Lars Andemening: no more than a clean skull when she stared across at him with her sleepy sidewise mouth?

He shouted, "Maybe you like it that they shot him dead in the streets! Maybe you have affectionate feelings for the S.S.! Nostalgia for the Gestapo!"

His head felt all skull. He watched her stand up, straining from the chair: an old woman.

"Prove you're your father's son," she commanded. "Why don't you prove it? I don't say prove he's a genius. I don't say prove his nouns and verbs. I say prove he's your father."

"I know his voice. I know his mind." A pressure of telling rose in him. He wanted to tell her that he knew his father's eye; but he did not.

"Why don't you pick Kafka to be the son of? Then people would have some recognition. They'd be impressed. They'd look around at you."

"I know who my father is. I know him inside out. I know more than anyone."

"You know him inside out," she sang. "You've collected him, you're a collector!"

"Sometimes," Lars said slowly, "his words come out of my mouth."

"You're a reviewer! You write reviews! Nobody gets the Nobel Prize for writing on Mondays!"

Very slowly he began to tell. A stone lay on his tongue; but he began. "When I wake up," he said heavily, "I can see my father's eye. It seems to be my eye, but it's his. As if he lets me have his own eye to look through."

"You want to resurrect him. You want to *be* him." She did not soften. "Mimicry. Posing in a mirror. What's the point of it? What will it bring you? You throw out your life."

"And your life?" The stone fell away. "If you think there's no point, how come *you're* in it? You're in it as much as I am. More. You've found all the best things. The letters. Everything from Warsaw. If it's not worth *my* while, how is it worth yours?"

"When Dr. Eklund's away it passes the time." She sank back under the lamp; she lifted her hand and switched it off. "Dr. Eklund warned me long ago against sleeping in daylight. It induces hallucinations. Poor Lars, you're a visionary. There's no *use* to it. If I didn't have my shop to keep me on my toes, I'd nap in the afternoon like you."

The last syllables swam into black space. A trickle of light from the street drifted through the mullioned door.

Lars came and hunched himself on the floor beside her.

"Do you want coffee?" she suddenly asked him.

"No."

"Take some vodka."

"No."

"Then you'd better go home. It's the middle of the night."

"I'm not coming back," he said.

A fragment of laughter scraped the darkness.

Lars said, "No, it's finished. What I get from you is mockery. Enough."

"You want to be taken on faith."

"Trust. I want trust."

"Vapor and smoke. Stories, letters—they're all someone's hallucination. How do you know you weren't born right here in Stockholm? An infant, smuggled! It's only a story. You don't know anything for sure. Your mother's a cloud, your father's a fog. There's nothing reliable in any of it."

"Except the shooting. You believe in *that*."

"Death's reliable."

She was all at once discomposed; she flung out her hands. The gesture of an oracle. He was astonished—she was surrendering her own old landscape, she was taking her turn. It was her life—the life before—she was giving him, out of the blue: the life before Dr. Eklund. She pressed it out in the swoop of two or three lines—her arms a line in the black air, the fence a row of black lines. It appeared before him in the dark with the clarified simplicity of a charcoal drawing—a predestined image. He followed the black lines, he traced her, there at the fence, heaving lumps over it to the shadows on the other side: as a young woman she had lived, she said, in a village not far from one of those camps, and crept at night as often as she could without detection to throw food over the fence. It was like a cage in there, crammed with dying beasts. She heard their scratchings, clawings, mufflings, muzzlings; they were all shadows; they were afraid to come near. She heard them tear into the paper wrappings; then they stuffed the wrappings into their sleeves, into their shoes; she heard them gulp and chew. Occasionally they vomited, or exploded, with cries like muzzled beasts, into floods of diarrhoea; she made out all this in the blind night by the sound and the pestilential smell. Often she heard shooting; there was no sense to the shooting, she could not tell where or why, it had no direction. Sometimes it seemed to come from between her own feet. And immediately after the war she picked up the daffodil lamp, only that, and a few old books, and traveled north across the border, leaving Germany behind. She would never go back. If she had a family there she did not mention it. In Stockholm she found Dr. Eklund and married him.

He had never seen her so excited. Something had provoked her. Her cheeks were drawn down—puffs of weighted dough; abruptly she had the look of a bulldog. He did not believe her; she was a liar. She wanted not to be what she had been before. It was more intuition than suspicion that he did not believe her: she knew too much about that fence—the other side of it, among the shadows. She knew what they did with the bits of paper—how they squashed every scrap inside their rags to make a lining against the cold, how they padded their shoes with it against the sores. She had strangely intimate views—they were like summonings—about the hunger and the vomiting and the bursting of the bowels. She summoned these with a votive memory. She summoned too well, too potently, too acutely: the night space beyond the fence could not account for so deep a summoning. He supposed she was one of them, but hidden—one of the shadows inside.

"You're a refugee," he said. "A survivor. Like me."

"Like you? You don't know what you are! Safe in Stockholm your whole life! You don't know *who* you are!" She let out that same unconfined newfangled laughter: doglike. "You'll say you're anything at all!"

"You were behind that fence. On the inside."

"The outside. I heard the shooting."

"You want to conceal it. You're afraid of being found out."

"Oh yes, a Marrano. Like your idea of the Queen, poor woman!"

"You don't want to admit it. You want to be rid of it. Your name," he accused—he had spied it written in one of those old books of hers. "I saw what your name used to be."

"There are plenty of Bavarian burghers called Simon. They're all Catholic."

"And what are you?"

"By religion? A bookseller."

"A refugee," he insisted, "like any refugee. You escaped. A survivor."

"Stockholm is full of survivors," she said; she was quiet now. She was obstinate. She was not going to yield. Instead, she held out her key. "Here, let yourself out. You'll come back, whatever you say."

"No. I'm not coming back. I told you."

She slid behind him to the door. The little fear he always had of her seemed to heat up the key as he turned it; then he relinquished it into her hand.

"You'll *want* to come back. Think what you've got on order! Poles and Czechs! Vaculík, Hrabel, Konwicki. Witold Gombrowicz! You might not want to come back for me, but for Konwicki, for Gombrowicz—"

He stepped out into the cold—she was still laughing back there, behind the door. Mockery. But it was so; for the sake of these he would return. He felt how she had overmastered him after all. He was glad to keep away. It might be weeks before she reeled him back, a helpless fish on her line, to fetch his order. All the time until then he would keep away; he would keep away with all his might. It came to him how desolate he was. He had imagined her entangled with him. It was the shooting, only the shooting, she was entangled with. His father's skeleton.

6

ON THE WEEKEND he went to visit Ulrika's mother. She lived in the suburbs, in a section beyond the city that had once been semi-rural and was now growing more and more Turkish. Ulrika's mother was proud of her house—it had been in the family, on the female side, for seven generations. The foundation was stone, the rest a rust-colored old brick. It struck Lars—for the first time—that Ulrika's hair had been just this color: brick dusted all over with powdery brown. Birgitta, his first wife, was an ordinary blonde. He had not heard anything about Birgitta in over a decade. She was married again and had two small children; he knew this much, but otherwise she almost never entered his mind. Ulrika he had once been bitter against, because she had taken his daughter away to America. But the bitterness was stale, and when Ulrika's mother in her confusion led him into the house he recognized that lately Ulrika too was seldom in his thoughts. Even his little daughter had begun to fade.

"Lars! You should tell me when you're coming. You should call, for heaven's sake!"

"I don't have a phone."

"You didn't use to be such a primitive. Look at me, a walking mud pie, look how I am, straight from the garden—"

"I've brought you something. My flat is so small I have no room to store anything."

Ulrika's mother's mouth suddenly pinched itself inward. It was a trick Lars recalled from Ulrika.

"I can't *keep* things for you, Lars. It isn't right. We aren't relations any more. Besides, Ulrika has an American sweetheart now. An engineer. He works for IBM."

"It's Karin's thing, not mine." He drew out a flat rectangular object from his briefcase and set it down between them on the parlor table. It was his daughter's old paint set.

"What am I supposed to do with that?"

"Put it away somewhere."

"It makes no sense to keep a baby thing like that. Next time I see Karin she'll be grown. I can show you her latest snapshots if you like—they came just last week. A big tall girl. All that black hair—she takes after you before you went gray. And look," she said, "the paint's all dried out, it's no good anyhow."

"It's been like that a long time."

"What do I want a dried-out piece of trash like that for?"

"A keepsake."

"Your idea of a keepsake, Lord help us! It's because you don't know what it is to inherit anything, Lars. I don't blame you. I've always felt for you."

"When Karin was tiny she already loved to paint," Lars said.

"All kids like to make messes."

This ignorant old widow. He thought of his father's drawings: *ready and waiting for us at the very beginning of life.* Is it possible that these predestined images can flow from generation to generation?—he remembered how certain phantomlike lines, wanton, curiously powerful and strong, had astonished him, sweeping out from his daughter's fierce little fist: the power of genes. Ulrika had taken small notice.

"I told Ulrika," Ulrika's mother said, "how hard it would be for her if she married an orphan. We're a family that's always had our own house. This same house you're sitting in, solid stone, good brick, if you want to talk about keepsakes! And a nice garden too. Ulrika, I said, we know who we are. We come from right here, and always have. I told her it would be like going with the gypsies to go with an orphan. It's not your fault, Lars. But it wasn't right for Ulrika. Don't think I didn't tell her! She ended up a gypsy herself. Lord knows when she'll find her way home again. Maybe never. By now she speaks American day and night and in her sleep. Karin in those pictures looks pure American, doesn't she? Those shoes! Ulrika shouldn't allow shoes like that. And that dark hair. I never thought I'd have a grand-child as dark as one of these Turks around here. They're every-where now, they've moved in on both sides next door. I can't work in my garden without some Turkish man watching. The women are worse."

He sat with her for another hour, tracing Ulrika in every one of her gestures—he had never observed this before. Now and then he stared down at the photographs of his daughter. It was evident that she was going to be tall, but otherwise he hardly knew her for his own. He was still unreconciled to her name— he who had chosen his own name, and out of the dictionary, like a spell! Karin: Ulrika had wanted this commonplace. Lars had dreamt of the Four Matriarchs. Rachel, Rebecca, Sarah, Leah. In the snapshots—he held them like a pack of cards, frivolously —Karin receded from him; she seemed no more than a plaster cast, with empty eyes. The original was elsewhere. In the photos she was older and coarser than the quick child whose paint set he meant to rid himself of. He might meet her again one day; or not. If she longed for him she would search him out. She would study his case if he deserved it. Even a child can become a scholar of loss. He wondered whether he ought to take the paint set back with him—Ulrika's mother would only toss it out, nothing could be plainer. But he left it behind.

7

IT WAS EASY to keep away from Heidi. He felt how easy.
Heidi was nothing to him. He had lost no one. Still, he was
plagued now and then by a heaviness, a thickness of the lung, an
inner lurch as glutinous as mourning.

He walked past the Academy and discovered that this density
of breathing, this viscosity, was only ordinary fury. Mrs. Eklund!
She was jealous: she had called him a collector and his father a
skeleton. *A doctor's wife considers you either a madman or a
phony*—this was from that last batch of letters Heidi had wangled
out of Warsaw: she had recited this insult with zest. "No doubt
a bad translation," she added, to be fair. He seized the Polish
original. The words did not change their spots. They belonged to
Witold Gombrowicz, one of his father's epistolary cronies. Six
years before the shooting (Heidi's count), Lars's father in an
open letter to the press had spat out his bitter rebuff to this
doctor's wife and her opinions: *Dear Witold . . . These are the
mass instincts that eclipse within us a clarity of judgment, rein-
troducing the archaic and barbaric epistemologies, the arsenal of
atavistic and bankrupt logic. . . . You side with inferiority.* The
poor doctor's wife, a woman Gombrowicz had run into on the
Number 18 streetcar, in 1936, on Wilcza Street. It was probably

true that Gombrowicz sided with her. She was exasperated: Lars's father was over her head. A madman or a phony. She condemned him for being beyond her. Barbaric epistemologies!

She must be an old woman by now, this doctor's wife Gombrowicz had met on the Number 18, as old as Jozefina, the fiancée; or dead. Gombrowicz, surly humorist, was also dead. *You side with inferiority.* Over the Academy, in the night sky, floating, wafting, aloft in the streaming snow, Lars saw, or almost saw, his father's body, not at all a skeleton—an incandescent apparition billowing with light, puffed out, the light stretching his father's skin to palest transparency. This balloon-father, shedding luminosity, light falling in sheets from his swollen body, drifted into the white flux and merged with it. First a blur, then a smudge, then a blankness: above the Academy's roof now there was only the shower of snow-hyphens brightly descending.

It was a Thursday night. At the *Morgontörn*, at Anders's desk in Anders's cubicle, Lars—rigid, electric, anxious—was typing his review for the next Monday: a novel by Danilo Kiš, translated from the Serbo-Croatian; and there was Gunnar hanging over him, teasing and prickling, and there was Anders just stepping out of the ancient elevator, breathing dragon steam, streaked and pocked with melting snow. Anders kicked off his galoshes and reached for his vodka. The little mice ran. Lars's page was stippled with errors. He began typing his first sentence all over again: *Here is a universe as confined as a trap, where the sole heroes are victims, where muteness is for the intrepid only.* A grand soliloquy—he was instantly sick of his words, trite, portentous, posturing. All gesture. A vertigo passed through Lars's head. The two of them, Gunnar and Anders, went spinning around him—a pair of desperate vaudevillians, rivals, Siamese twins. They had their old show: cavorting and caviling, nipping at each other and at Lars. Anders handed Lars a scrap—it was Heidi calling him back. She wanted him, she was surrendering.

But the note, scribbled off the telephone by the *Morgontörn's* somnolent receptionist, was no more than a garble. MRS. EKLUND PHONED ABOUT YOUR SISTER. That fool of a girl downstairs. Lars, in the corridor, obediently filled Anders's kettle at the tap. In Anders's cubicle, Gunnar was chirping *confined as a trap, where the sole heroes are victims*, and all the rest. It shamed Lars. He could not be angry at these interesting sufferers, but he felt himself without weight in the world, a molecule bobbing along in a sluice. "Gentlemen," he said, "I'm off," and trudged out to retrieve his Czechs and Poles at Heidi's shop.

8

ACROSS THE SQUARE, over the Academy, his father's bloated shape had long ago disintegrated among the gray steeples and the snow spilling slantwise. A smell of something roasting, what was that? He crossed the bridge over the locks, where the salty Baltic squalled under his feet. He had kept away a good three weeks. Heidi let him cool his heels before coming to the door.

"You smell like a rutting sheep," she complained. He was sweating from his rapid walk—nearly a run—in the new snow. His boots were dripping. She made him leave them in the vestibule; she grumbled that he was interrupting—she was hard at work, a big shipment had arrived that very day. But he saw from her long slow helpless yawn that the knock of his penknife on the glass had just now awakened her. She was spending the night on the cot in the back room. Dr. Eklund was somewhere else; it seemed to Lars that she was embarrassed by this.

"Nobody but you wants such stuff," she told him—it was, this remark, a commonplace with her. Vaculík, Hrabel, Gombrowicz, Konwicki. She piled up his order on her little back-room table. "What names! Didn't I say these fellows would fetch you back?" She yawned again, but with a certain willed smugness. "Why didn't you come last week? When I phoned?"

"Anders picked up your message from the receptionist's desk an hour ago," Lars said.

"An hour ago? That paper you work for! They'd be a week behind in reporting the end of the world." A wild alertness took hold of her. "You're too late, by days. I thought you'd have the sense to get here right away. I kept her waiting that whole afternoon."

"Who was that?"

"A woman with an interest in Polish."

She was being wary, tricky. In his three weeks away he had not forgotten how dangerous she could be, how she could topple him.

"If the Princess wants me back," he said, "*she's* too late. She threw me out when I thought I still needed her. I've got no use for her now," but he recognized in his own croak—swallowing down the bit of vodka Heidi had given him when he asked for it—that something new lay between them.

"No, no, not Mrs. Rozanowska. I told them who at the *Morgontörn*. I *told* them. They said they'd put it in the message. My God, Lars, if you had your own phone in your own flat like an ordinary person—"

He pulled out the wadded-up square Anders had brought him and looked at it. MRS. EKLUND PHONED ABOUT YOUR SISTER. The snow had somehow crept into his pocket and dampened everything in it. The preposterous words had begun to run. "I haven't *got* a sister. There's no sister anywhere in it at all. You know that."

"That's probably true. I didn't think she *was* your sister. It smelled fishy to me from start to finish." Heidi formulated one of her calculating scowls—she was all scandalous bliss. "I don't say there wasn't a resemblance, but the fact is she hasn't come back. She said she'd come back and she hasn't. I asked her to leave it for you but she wouldn't. I don't blame her, if it's genuine."

"Leave what? If what's genuine?"

"My dear boy"—she had never before addressed him this way, him with his graying head! but there was an importance in it that penetrated—"she has the manuscript of *The Messiah* in a little white plastic bag. She carries it around like that. The original. The thing itself. I saw it with my own eyes."

"*The Messiah*? No one has that. It disappeared. It doesn't exist."

"She's got it in her bag."

"*Who* has, for God's sake?"

"Your sister."

"There isn't any sister. A fraud. You've been taken in."

"She didn't *say* she was your sister. I only drew a conclusion."

"You drew a conclusion!" he howled.

"Well, if she calls herself the daughter of the author of *The Messiah*, and you're the *son* of the author of *The Messiah*, that makes her your sister. It stands to reason."

"It stands to reason! The daughter! There isn't any daughter! There isn't any *Messiah*!"

"Not so long ago you had a different opinion."

"The manuscript's gone, there's no one alive who thinks anything else."

"You said yourself it might have been hidden."

"Whoever had it was taken away. Whoever had it is dead."

"*She* isn't dead. She told me the reason she's got it is just because she *is* his daughter. No one else could have gotten hold of it. It was saved explicitly for her."

Lars said, "There's no room in the story for another child. It's not feasible. It can't be. You know the story as well as I do. There's only me."

"Well, maybe there's you and maybe there's not. And if there's you, why can't there be another one?"

"What did she *say*? What exactly?"

"That the man who wrote *The Messiah* was her father."

"But he's *my* father!" Lars cried.

Heidi beamed out a rascally gleam. "If the manuscript doesn't exist, and the daughter doesn't exist—"

"You know there's no daughter."

"—then maybe there's no son either."

"I'm here. Here I am."

"That's just what *she* said. A biblical annunciation. And every bit as convinced of it as you."

Wearing a white beret. Not too distant from Lars's own age, judging from the hair, which was just beginning to whiten, though only on one side of a slightly archaic middle part; the face was as clear as a baby's. There certainly *was* a resemblance, not acute—she wasn't a twin—but ripe, somehow, with hints. The similarities were in the absences, in the sort of look she *didn't* have. She didn't look content. She didn't look—well, *normal.* These negative hints made Heidi pay attention, though not right away—Heidi was on the watch for Dr. Eklund. Dr. Eklund was returning momentarily from Copenhagen. The woman had come in out of the blue—out of the snow—with her white plastic bag. Heidi kept her eye on it—shoplifters carry such things. But the woman didn't go near the bookshelves at all; she turned in the aisles and turned again. The shop had a wild morning brightness: snow-dazzle freakishly shot through with slashes of early sunlight, too sharp to bear. All that exaggerated whiteness seemed to be crowding into the narrow vestibule of the shop, and had swept the woman straight through the doorway. She asked the Turkish boy for the proprietor—it was the proprietor she wanted, because of those heaps of foreign books in the window. The foreign books had lured her; she had never noticed this shop before. She was used to walking all over Stockholm, but she was still new to it. You could tell from her accent how new. She had something astonishing, something stupendous, in her bag. Was there anyone here—perhaps even the proprietor—who could read Polish? Or who had access to the local Polish intelligentsia? In this very bag, the one in her hand (it was light enough, it wasn't a big tome), lay the work of a genius who happened—she wasn't going to be shy about this, she wouldn't hide *his* light under a bushel!—who happened to be her own father. Dead. Murdered. A victim, long ago, but immortal. And she was the daughter. *Here I am!* She had inherited her father's last known manuscript, a masterpiece the whole world believed to be wiped out, erased, vanished. It deserved translation into Swedish; she couldn't do this herself. It deserved translation into every language on the face of the earth. A visionary thing—the title itself showed how visionary—oh, amazing, it couldn't be explained in only half a minute. Was it possible the proprietor might know someone who could *do* something for a manuscript like this? Redeem it, accord it salvation, spread it like a gospel? The point was she was looking for a translator.

"So you offered her the Princess," Lars bit off.

"I offered her you."

"What are you talking about? What did you tell her?"

"I told her you're awash in Polish. I told her it's under your skin, not that you speak it like a native, but if anyone was ever possessed! I told her you're a madman for literature. I told her you're a connoisseur of the author of *The Messiah*. I told her all that."

"But not the deep fact. Not that."

"It's your secret, isn't it? You keep on keeping it, except when you spill it. How would I tell what you don't tell? The trouble is you have no confidence in me."

"If she had an accent—" He swallowed it down. "What kind of accent?"

"How do I know? I have an accent myself."

"The name, then. She gave her name."

"Elsa. No, Adela. I think it was Adela. Don't pester me

with such things, Lars. I *tried* to reach you, after all. I left that message with the *Morgontörn*, what more could I do? And then I made her stay and stay. She got sick of waiting and went off, do you blame her?"

"Where does she live?"

"She never told."

"Didn't she leave a phone number?"

"She said she would just rather come back."

"But she hasn't. Not in a week. We've lost her, and she's a crazy fraud—"

"*Some*thing was in that bag."

"It wasn't *The Messiah*."

"Then why should you care if we've lost her?"

There was an exhaustion between them now, as if they had just run out of a burning house. The roasting smell trickled up out of Lars's clothes: it fumed up from his belly, his armpits, the soaked pockets on his rump, his snow-dampened feet. Heidi's gleam was an ember. Her mouth relapsed to sleepiness. Lars wondered whether, with all her talent for turning things askew, she had given over his story—his deep fact—to Dr. Eklund; or whether she had given over her own story. The fence. She had, in the last moment, revived their old habit of "we"—this hadn't escaped him. But she couldn't be depended on: it occurred to him that the woman in the white beret, in the morning's white brilliance, carrying a featherweight *Messiah* in a white bag, was, if she wasn't an angel, a lie.

"Something's burning," he said.

"Oh God! The stove. Go and see, Lars. I suppose I never shut the flame under this afternoon's pot. I'm getting to be an old woman."

He took two steps. "The fire's off. It wasn't turned on."

"Then it's the smell of glue. The binding glue in that new shipment. Sometimes it smells like that. Or else it's you. Sweat. A rutting sheep. Smog." She was dimming, failing, a light dying out. Something was snuffing her. "The roof of the snow pressing down. It keeps the smoke on the ground. In the streets. Every chimney in the city sending out smoke—"

"It could be the chimneys," he agreed. A quirk of the atmosphere. Meteorology. Stockholm smoldering at the northernmost margins of the industrial West, houses in clusters, spires like an army of bayonets, office blocks, factories, flats, computers, the grit-filled mists of habitation, hesitation, wear, use, decay, loss. The bad smell behind that fence. Even the wake of angels. The white wings of angels passing in flocks are known to release the odor of burning feathers.

He thought of his little fear. "Dr. Eklund," he said, "when did he get back from Copenhagen?"

"He's not back yet. Look at the roads, for heaven's sake. Planes don't take off in heavy weather."

"Wasn't that conference over long ago?"

"What conference?"

"The one in Copenhagen."

"It wasn't a conference. You've got Copenhagen mixed up with somewhere else. A consultation. The prima ballerina of the Danish ballet. She wouldn't perform. Wouldn't set foot on the stage."

"Dr. Eklund's not in Copenhagen," Lars said.

"Well, maybe not. Lord knows where he's been stranded. You can never be sure."

She drifted toward her cot. She wanted her cot; she was old and full of sleep. She wanted him to go. But he persisted—he could feel how his teeth tore into it: "Dr. Eklund," he said, "isn't stranded anywhere."

She was, he noticed, wearing slippers. She dropped them off under the daffodil and handed him her key. "Lock up when you leave. You can bring this back next time." Next time: she was expecting him to resume. She had never before entrusted him with the key—she meant him to take it away with him. He watched her strain as she bent to roll down her stockings, gartered at the knees; then she fell back on the disheveled cot. White strings of her hair blew off the pillow. She widened her mouth for another yawn; her eyes watered. "If he isn't stranded, then he's on his way."

"Mrs. Eklund."

Her face was in the pillow. Her voice was drawing itself out, thinner and thinner. It was dissolving. "Be sure to get that key back here pretty soon. It's one of Dr. Eklund's extras. It isn't that he loses them. He leaves them places. At the hospital. In the flat."

Lars said steadily, "You're all alone here every night. There isn't any flat. There isn't any Dr. Eklund."

"Go away. Take your books and go. I need to sleep. I'm asleep."

"Dr. Eklund's a phantom."

"No, no, you don't follow, you don't see," she soughed into the pillow. "She's dancing again. The prima ballerina."

The key was heating up in his hand. "A refugee impostor," he said. "That's what you are."

In the little vestibule, Czechs and Poles in his arms, he struggled back into his boots, teetering on one leg at a time and leaning against the glass of the display window. It was just where she had stood—the so-called daughter—with her white plastic bag. In which rested, or swarmed in chaos, certain sheets of manuscript, whatever they were. In the window the enameled Royal Family were still tucked benignly into their sofas, and the sea gulls were speckling Lake Vänern, and alongside were those towering piles of Russians and South Americans and Englishmen, so many foreign urgencies babbling. The key went straight into the lock without difficulty in the broad circle of light that looped out from the streetlamp. In this spot she—the so-called daughter—had determined to declare herself. *Here I am.*

"He's on his way," he heard Heidi call from the back room. A moan: or not exactly a moan. Rather, the sound of indecipherable syllables evaporating at the bottom of the sea. German? Polish? Serbo-Croatian? A foreign babble, unintelligible. He put the key in his pocket. It burned against his thigh. His little fear. And then he thought: look! it doesn't burn, it isn't burning. There is no Dr. Eklund. Dr. Eklund doesn't exist. Dr. Eklund is a phantom. *Reality is as thin as paper and betrays with all its cracks its imitative character.* Now he was not sure whether Heidi had called out anything at all. He was, anyhow, already yards away from the shop. But his little fear was cooled. His little fear was gone.

9

H E D E C I D E D , the next day, to forgo his afternoon quilt. He headed instead for the *Morgontörn*; it was the first time in months he had seen the place in light. It was business, it was the world, it was movement—they were putting out the paper. It went on like this, telephones and shouts and typewriters, until the secretaries left for home—an office boy flashing by with a long noodle of galleys, the stutter of someone's typing clacking out of one of the cubicles; Nilsson yelling: something was missing, something was late. There was a common energy—the intermittent vowels in the floorboards weren't the least bit ghostly, and the noise of it all ground together had the unitary drive of an organism out on its own: God knew what the name of such a single-minded animal might be. Nothing spooky. A big nosy dog. Lars didn't take note of any mice. No doubt they were confined to barracks.

"Lars! What are you doing here?" Nilsson gave him a bossy thump and raced on through the roil. It was a thing to marvel at, the book department in daylight—how the sun, moonlike, wan, wintry, grainy and fickle, more gray than pale, cut out patches everywhere. The strangeness of these sun-pockets: windows! A vague electric bulb and the usual scratchings and scrapings against the shaft kept the elevator in its shabby night, but otherwise the chairs and desks and file cabinets had the look of life. Over in a corner the gang of three-o'clock gossips were well into it, Gunnar and Anders among them. Lars was surprised, and then, on second thought, he wasn't. Night prowlers somewhat on his own style, they gargled with what was what and who was where and why—it meant they had to come to the well, now and then, for water.

He was breathing through a veil—a sort of stupor or trance. It was the habit of the quilt; at this hour he was used to his nap. The rims of his eyes itched and bothered: a pair of old hoops he had bumped through too many ditches. He was wakeful enough, but with a ragged edge; a buzz; a recklessness. He felt somehow abused—he didn't care what anyone said. He nudged himself nearer; no one acknowledged him, no one lifted a shoulder to let him in. They were telling a translation story—how Sven Strömberg, in an absent moment, pushing to meet a deadline on an Australian novel and meaning to engage the word "trust," inadvertently transmuted it to "trussed," and tied up his faithful heroine in knots. "You can't pin it on Sven, it could happen to anyone. All those puns and homonyms." "Homer nodding." "Freud. A psychological substitution." "You forget that Sven Strömberg doesn't *have* a psyche." "So what's he keep in that paunch?" "Some sort of cheese. You can smell it on his breath." "It isn't *cheese* that's on his breath." "At least his howlers are his own, nothing's swiped."

Laughter. "Has anyone seen Flodcrantz?" "I heard he ran to Finland to hide out." "He's got the shakes. Even his ears. His knuckles. My God, last I had a look at him the man was a jelly." "It's his own doing. He asked for it." "They say he's suicidal." "That Olof? He takes vitamins!" "Well, he wanted to be talked about. It's better than getting buried every week on the culture page." "He's made himself famous. He's relishing the whole business." "His hand quivers. His chin." "It's an act. He's an actor. The greatest Thespian of them all." "Please, the fellow's suffering. He's sick. He's not normal."

And on and on. It was this month's scandal. A reviewer at one of the evening papers, an admired (some said dangerously envied) younger poet who had just published his second collection of verse, had been exposed—by Sven Strömberg, of all people!—as a plagiarist. Every single poem in Olof Flodcrantz's new book was a purloined translation of the work of a different American poet. Flodcrantz had actually been shameless enough to include, among the safer unknowns, a few stanzas by Robert Frost that Sven Strömberg had himself translated a dozen years ago for an anthology remaindered six weeks after publication: *Bards of the New World*. The most captivating circumstance in the story was its luckless climax—how Sven Strömberg had uncovered the crime against all odds, since he was celebrated for never reading anything he wasn't being paid to read. On the other hand, he was also celebrated for lapping up the most impudent syrups of flattery, so when Olof Flodcrantz sent—*sent!* —a copy of the criminal volume, eloquently inscribed, to Sven Strömberg, and when Sven Strömberg took in the inscription naming him the foremost man of letters in the nation, it was natural enough for Sven Strömberg (a courteous man) to return the compliment by endorsing Olof Flodcrantz's newest lucubrations. "Purely original," he wrote to Olof; "purely original," he said to everyone he ran into. Sven's confirmation of Olof's pure originality had already been well circulated in the stewpot when, thumbing through the pages to gaze once again on Olof's pleasing inscription, Sven Strömberg happened to come on the familiar lines by Robert Frost. In his own translation. Pirated; usurped.

The most delectable shock of the season so far. The three-o'clock gossips—it was now nearer five o'clock—turned it this way and that, testing for motives, for consequences. Who had duped whom? Mad Olof!—putting his head in the lion's mouth, but only after first waking up the lion. Yet the poor lion was hardly in a position to bite. Was it a case of rage, malice, revenge, despair? Or—"Contrariwise," said Gunnar—puckishness, camp, comedy, dada? A postmodernist plot. Sven was behind it all: it was Sven who had dug up for Olof all those Americans cleverly named Robert. Creeley and Mezey and Bly! Lowell, Penn Warren, Graves. Anders would have nothing to do with this theory of looking under beds for the culprit. A solemn accident of reformist patriotism, whatever the intent. Just what we need, showing us up for what we are, rubbing our noses in the doll-house dust. Ultimate ironic burlesque of Swedish parochialism. Exposure, once and for all, of the littleness of the life of letters in decrepit old Stockholm.

"Crocodiles! Earn your keep," Nilsson yelled, running by. The secretaries were going home. The moonlike sun had faded in the windows. It was the stewpot at full boil.

"Well, there's something else," Lars said. No one heard. They had moved on to Olof Flodcrantz's fate at his paper, whether he would be fired or kept on as a culture hero. He was, whatever else you thought of him, daring—you had to admit he had brio: all those Roberts! Not to mention the blurring of borders, of property lines. Internationalism versus the local pond. Socialism in the ideal—the text's the thing, never mind who sets it down. Shakespeare by any other name. A narrow moralist might speak of theft, but what was it if not the halo of the universal that the whole planet strains toward? Non-exclusive loveliness going from hand to hand among the nations. The fool in the case was Sven Strömberg—showing up the impostor, even at the price of his own dignity. How ludicrous the leap from "purely original" to "Stop, thief!"—everything turns on whose ox is gored: there you are.

In spite of which, not one of them would mind it if Olof Flodcrantz got fired.

Thus the stewpot in the early winter dark. Cigarette smoke

like torn nets hanging. All over the world the great ladle was stirring, stirring. The poets, dreamers, thinkers, hacks. The ambitious and the meditative. The opportunists and the provocateurs. The cabalists and the seducers. This stewpot—these hot tides—Lars under his quilt a short walk away had shut out, week after week: for the sake of catching sight of his father's eye. His father too had shunned the stewpot. Drohobycz instead of Warsaw, Drohobycz instead of Paris, Drohobycz instead of anywhere.

"Deadlines, gentlemen!" Nilsson yelled, flying past; he had on his coat and muffler. The tight little cluster loosened, and out from the middle of it serenely stepped, or was mildly ejected, the *Morgontörn*'s only literary woman, in her man's shirt and tie, saluting Lars with two fingers raised, one with a blackened writer's bump. She was rumored to be Sven Strömberg's lover of twenty years' standing; she had not spoken a syllable in his defense—her voice anyhow had the brittle electronic character of an official interpreter—but her small sly mouth was rich with a certain moist-looking sweetness. There was a sweetness in all of them, the whole three-o'clock crew—the weak honey of reverence. Literary creatures who served, sidestepped, and sometimes sold out the Muses. Their so-called scandals, their scramblings, their feuds, their polymorphous life in the stewpot: how innocent, how distant from the palaces of live thunder, how weak they were before the altar of Lars's father's unmoving eye. Now they were putting on their padded jackets, fur hats, fleece boots; it seemed to Lars they were snubbing him, or else they were oblivious—here was Gunnar rushing by, and then Anders, hurrying toward wives, stepfathers, aunts, groaning elderly households. The stewpot was breaking up. The *Morgontörn* was beginning to take on its rickety nighttime mien.

"Wait," Lars called again, "there's something else."

They were streaming past him, some toward the bottleneck in front of the elevator, most down the grunting wooden stairs. The poor old *Morgontörn*, collapsing backward—into the last century, into night, into decay. Already the mice were preparing to emerge; you could hear them drilling in phalanxes behind the walls.

Lars ran to the top of the stairwell and called down, "Something else! News!"

Sven Strömberg's lover, hitching her sailor's coat over her shirt and tie, stopped on the landing.

Lars called, "*The Messiah*'s turned up! Here! In Stockholm!"

Clatter on the steps; chatter; rumblings. "It's Lars Andemening," Sven Strömberg's lover explained to the landing below. "I think he's announcing the Second Coming."

"Don't tell me Olof Flodcrantz is back from Finland?" someone hooted up. "That soon?"

Laughter up and down the stairs.

"His daughter's got the manuscript. It's *found*," Lars called.

"What manuscript?"

Lars leaned over the rail. In the twilight of all those flights of stairs a thousand flickering faces were lifting toward him. "*The Messiah*," he called. "The lost *Messiah* of Bruno Schulz."

"Stockholm rumors. The world's hotbed."

"That Pole? He never had a daughter."

"If you've never heard of it, leave it to Lars."

"Or if it's dead."

"No, no, everybody's dead. Tolstoy. Ibsen. Even Strindberg. It gets to Lars only if it's to-tal-ly obscure."

"If it never existed."

"If you *wish* it never existed."

"Lars!" This was Anders, halfway down. "Cat's out of the bag. All that resurrecting you do. All those unknowns and esoterics raised from the grave—"

Sven Strömberg's lover said neatly, "Lars Andemening, the Messiah of Stockholm."

"Crocodiles!" Nilsson yelled up. "Always after a sensation."

At the bottom of the staircase Lars met Nilsson waiting for

him. "The telephone girl handed me this a second before quitting time. I ran into her coming out of the ladies' room. Why don't you get yourself a phone at home, Lars? The staff here isn't your butler. I'm not your valet."

Lars read: MRS. EKLUND PHONED. DR. EKLUND BACK. PLEASE RETURN KEY.

He pressed, "But you know what it signifies—if *The Messiah*'s found."

"One more book in the world," Nilsson said, "that isn't *Pippi Longstocking*. People complain, Lars—your reviews are practically theology. A little more wholesomeness for Monday, how about it? Soft-pedal the surreal, go easy on the existential dread, how about it? Give it a try."

Lars had entered the stewpot and it had vomited him up.

10

IN THE MORNING the snow was brownish in the roads, and tire-marked. There were heaps of it, in waist-high banks, at the sidewalk's edge. Walking was easy and light. Lars arrived at Heidi's shop so quickly that he had no time to notice his mood. He noticed it only when he looked all around for Heidi and instead came on the Turkish boy raising the feather duster to his shoulder like a sentry with a rifle. Mrs. Eklund was out. "You take this for her then," Lars told the Turkish boy, holding out the key. The Turkish boy demurred: *he* wasn't supposed to have any key, and if he was allowed to watch the shop at all it was because there were no real customers (clearly Lars wasn't one of *these*) at this hour anyhow.

Lars drifted back into the street. What was this exulting? It was nearly ten o'clock: he tried to imagine where Heidi might be. She was not in her flat; she had no flat. She was not with Dr. Eklund; Dr. Eklund was a phantom. What was this exulting? The delirium of what he had done! He had proclaimed the return of his father's lost last book. The stewpot's disbelief, their indifference, what was that? He hardly credited it himself. And the daughter! There was no daughter, and still he had proclaimed her, in order to proclaim the risen *Messiah*.

He had nowhere to go, so he headed for his flat. He wondered whether he ought to worry about Nilsson's "Give it a try" —was it a warning? Would Nilsson, who had hired him and who was in a way his protector—would Nilsson throw him out? For the sins of unwholesomeness, theology, surrealism, existential dread? Or for the larger sin of unpopularity? He might work at enlivening his style—Gunnar, for instance, peppered his columns with *slow motion, back alley, big deal, wisecrack,* even *so what.* Anders called all these expressions "Velveetisms"; a truly cosmopolitan mind, he said, wouldn't stoop to such vulgarities. But Lars remembered a passage in one of his father's tales concerning *a great theater of illusion, a magnificent wax figure exhibition,* that once came to Drohobycz: *No, they were not authentic Dreyfuses, Edisons, or Lucchenis; they were only pretenders. They may have been real madmen, caught red-handed at the precise moment a brilliant* idée fixe *had entered their heads. . . . Ever since then, that one idea remained in their heads like an exclamation mark, and they clung to it, standing on one foot, suspended in midair.* Gunnar Hemlig and Anders Fiskyngel, waxwork men. The *Morgontörn,* a wax museum. Even the mice were artificial, operated by hidden motors in the walls.

What a tenderness he felt—this exulting that had hold of him!—for their wax faces, wax eyes with (this was odd) wax tears of pain or reproach or deprivation: Gunnar and Anders and Sven Strömberg's lover with her curly wax tie and even Nilsson, all of them wax exhibits connected to wires by buttons at the coccyx, or else invisibly controlled by distant wireless computers. Their terrible helplessness. One idea remained like an exclamation mark in the sweet-tasting pink wax of their heads: the stewpot, the stewpot! While here, *here*—Lars had reached the door of his flat, and was fingering his key—here in his own startled bed, under his tossed and tangled quilt, his father's eye, lit, steady, unmoving, strong and blatant, a violent white ray, was spilling out the wilderness of God. A vivid bestiary strangely abundant, discharging the white light of plenitude, and they turned from it, they shunned it, if they did not deride it they were remote from it, the greased beak had never seized them, no apparition, no sphere, no egg, no globe, no ultimate and forcing eye. He was forcing the key into the door; his own door—it did not fit. Then he understood it was the wrong key—it was the key to Heidi's shop, so he fluttered inside his pocket to find his own.

He lived on the ground floor, just off a minuscule hallway cut from an angle of the wall. There was a diseased old leather chair out there, with a cracked leg, that a doctor had once set down in that spot, long ago, for the purpose of receiving certain large parcels. No one knew what was in them, except that it meant the doctor was rich—the house had seen better days, magical deliveries: enormous frosted cakes, ladies' hats plumed and ribboned, birds in cages. This fabled chair gave its characteristic squeal, and from around the corner, out of the little hallway, came a woman wearing a white beret.

"Mrs. Eklund told me where you live. If," she said, "you're the right one?"

She was carrying the white plastic bag.

"Lars Andemening? You can do Polish? You don't look Swedish."

The last one to say this to him—that he didn't look Swedish —was his foster mother; he was then sixteen. It made him run away: he had not yet learned whose son he was.

"I'm a refugee."

She showed no surprise. "All right, let's start"—she walked straight past him into his tiny flat; there was his bed, there was his crumpled wild quilt. It was more than a year since another human being had stood in this place. He was humiliated. Or else he did not know what he was. He was ashamed, frenetic. He rushed around to sweep some clothes off a chair. He cleared the table with a lightning arm. He was exposed, he was fearful; he was exulting.

"Mrs. Eklund told you to come here?"

"Because you don't have a telephone."

"You wouldn't leave your own number. You wouldn't say where you live."

"I have to be careful, don't I?"

"Careful of what?" he asked.

"Of what I'm in charge of." She gave her bag a shake. "I have an impulsive nature—I need to watch myself. I've spent a couple of weeks now watching *you*. I've been getting a point of view."

He was preoccupied by her accent. Did she sound like the Princess? But even the Princess was not so confident.

"Mrs. Eklund told me where to look. Mondays in the *Morgontörn*. I've been trying you out. You *know* things. If you can do it I'll take you."

"Do what?"

Now she was sitting on the edge of his bed. "I want a translator."

"I'm not a translator," Lars said. "I've never done any of that kind of thing."

"You Swedish intellectuals do everything. Mrs. Eklund says Stockholm is filled with literary virtuosos. History professors who do criticism, critics who do translations, every sort of linguist—"

"I'm not anything like that."

"Mrs. Eklund says you are."

"She's not qualified. She's nobody. She runs a bookshop, what's that? She wants to make fun of me, that's all."

"Why?"

He dangled Heidi's key. "Revenge. I've unlocked her secrets. I know all about her. She isn't what she seems."

Again the woman shook her bag. A witch with a rattle. "Revenge and illusion! You're just the one I want. Mrs. Eklund says you're crazy for the Polish writers."

"You shouldn't rely on her."

"Everyone important comes into her shop. One of her customers is actually a Princess. She gets all the professors—the intelligentsia. The Academy orders from her, did you know that?"

"Don't be so quick," he said. "You've only just met her."

"That's right," she agreed. "It went quick, quick! I think she's clairvoyant. She sees through walls. She saw through *me*, it didn't take her a minute—she understood even before I explained. She understood it all. Most people don't. Most people haven't heard of it. Not even the literary ones."

She pulled off her beret. She meant to settle in for a visit. It was true, it was just as Heidi had described it; she was graying, like himself. Sad streaks of grime like old slush. She looked to be his own age, or near it, but when she lifted her chin and he caught the plane of her flat cheek, a momentary child flashed out. She had that in common with him: that suddenly simplified gaze, as if some long-ago movie reel were running fleetingly through. He warned himself to be vigilant. Between her eyes—blackish-brown like his own—there were two well-established vertical trenches. Vigilance! She was not his sister; he had no sister.

"Most people don't know anything about any of it," she said.

His breath was trapped in his throat. "It isn't really *The Messiah*."

"Mrs. Eklund told you, didn't she? She told you what I've got."

"No one will ever believe you."

"You will."

"Is it in that bag? Not in that bag!" A foolishness: how foolish he was; but the unfamiliar jubilation quickened.

"Yes, yes, right here"—and shook it. The sound of fifty wings.

"It should be in a library," he said. "It should be in a vault. It should be somewhere safe."

"It's safe with me. It's mine. I'm in charge of it."

"You're not afraid of theft? You've made copies?"

"Copies?" Contempt: a voice of contempt. "If I brought you a copy, would you believe in it?"

"How can I believe anything?" Lars said. "You haven't got any credentials, you come out of nowhere—"

"Oh, credentials." And again he was puzzled by her accent, with its odd sibilances. "I'll give you my name."

"Adela."

"Adela, is that enough? That's only what Mrs. Eklund said. Don't you want the rest of it? Don't you want where I was born, and all about my parents, my education, all of that? I've *had* an education, whatever people think."

"I want to see what's in that bag," Lars said.

"It'll break your heart, the look of it. The condition it's in. Some of these pages I had to pull out of a pair of shoes."

"Shoes!"

"They were just stuffed in there, way in. In the toes, after a rain. To keep the shape. Have you ever been to Drohobycz?"

"No," Lars said.

"Warsaw?"

"No."

"I was born in Brazil, did you realize that? No one's told you *that*. In São Paulo. My mother ran there in the middle of the war. *You* call yourself a refugee! She was only fifteen and pregnant, it wasn't easy to get passage—she managed it without a visa, she's a crafty type. She makes friends, that's how she does it. And then she got used to it—living all over. People say we're bedouins."

"A pair of *shoes?*" Lars said.

"They belonged to this old woman in Warsaw. We've lived in São Paulo, Amsterdam, Budapest, Brussels. Then Warsaw. The place we stayed the longest was Warsaw. My mother grew up in Poland, she speaks Polish best. So do I, except for Portuguese. Six months ago we went to Grenoble, we all went, don't ask me why. It's just the way my mother is—"

"All? Are you a tribe, your mother and you?"

She colored a little. "She actually *married* someone down there—a funny Frenchman, I don't like him—so I came here. My Swedish is really good, isn't it? Good grasp of idiom—lots of people tell me that. Don't you think my Swedish is good? Well, it's not good enough. Not for revenge and illusion! Heaven help us, your bed's an act of God, an avalanche."

"Please, the table, on the table, not there—"

But she had already turned the white plastic bag upside down. A cascade of papers spilled over the humps and ridges of his quilt.

His father's handwriting. The writing—the letters—growing out of his father's true hand. Crossed-out words all over. He pitied each one: discarded, canceled, exiled. A beast—a sort of ape—began to jump inside his frame, from rib to rib: could it only be this pump, this pump of a heart? An inward ape heaving itself about. Beating with its fists, crashing. Exultation! And pity, pity. These old sheets, his father's poor old foolscap, had been through water, he saw. Wrinkled dead skins, rubbed, creased, drowned.

"They've gotten wet," he said.

"Their cellar was flooded once. The woman with the shoes— she was only a peasant woman, her husband delivered milk—"

"In Warsaw?" The ape, blind and berserk.

"In Drohobycz. A man in a long black coat paid the husband to dig under their cellar in the middle of the night. You know the kind of flat metal box men's garters used to be sold in? Long ago? The papers were in one of those. A drygoods box, the husband buried it under the cellar floor. The man in the coat said he would come back for it when the war was over and pay them some more, but he never did."

The Messiah: those scattered bruised pages. Leaves and leavings, nullified. Swallowed up. And resurrected now, on his own bed! The bed of rebirth—where, a hundred times before, the greased beak had seized him and thrust him under his father's terrible eye.

"It's enough," Lars said. "It's not the point."

"Don't you want to hear credentials? You said credentials. It's how I got the manuscript."

"I don't care about how. It's why. Why should you have it? Who are you to have it?"

"He gave it to me. The husband."

"He gave it to you in Drohobycz?"

She spread her arms as wide as geography. "Not the Drohobycz husband. The Warsaw husband."

The north light, knifing through his narrow window—he *had* a window, an archer's slit—sent a bright scimitar across his bed: the light was too cold, too sharp. A winter sharpness coursed like a spray of icicles over the peaks and valleys of his quilt. Her arms, stretched out, were contriving a cloud over his father's words. His father's words, under her shadow.

"You won't let me *tell* it," she argued.

And told: she went on telling it—it didn't occur to Lars to disbelieve or believe. Here was *The Messiah*; here. It was here. He thought of that. The story went on: he believed it, he didn't believe it. How the woman's husband died of a stroke, after the war, when there were no more Jews in Drohobycz. Deported, perished. All the Jews, all the hasidim in their long black coats —gassed, undone. How the man in the long black coat never came back to fetch the box. How the box had gone out of the woman's head—she was only a peasant woman, what was it to her? Her head was busy with selling her little house, no bigger than a hut, with a cellar that was damp and easy to dig up; then she went off to Warsaw to get work. In Warsaw she became a domestic, what else could she do? The box was left in Drohobycz, under the earth—she didn't give it a thought, why should she? The man in the long black coat never came back. It was the new people, the people who had bought the house—well, the cellar had a dirt floor, they started to lay cement down there, and the pickaxe threw up the box with its papers. They imagined it was a will when they opened it, a Jew's will, and they set out to find the woman in Warsaw, supposing she would reward them for restoring the papers; the papers might mean something; they might mean a legacy. The Jews when they went away left their valuables behind, everyone knew this—sometimes even their pots, pots with false bottoms, in which they hid their gold. But by then, in Warsaw, the woman had married again, she had a new husband and had moved away, to a brand-new flat on the other side of the city, in the rebuilt neighborhood where the Ghetto had stood. Where the Ghetto had fallen. Clean new flats in that place, no one could tell anything at all from the looks of it; the Ghetto was buried and gone; it was a nice new neighborhood.

"The woman told you all this?"

"The husband. When I came there it was much later, the woman was dead, she had died. That's how I came there, because she died in Tosiek Glowko's kitchen. His wife's kitchen. Tosiek Glowko was my mother's special friend all the time we lived in Warsaw. All my mother's special friends are younger— she can't help it, that's how she is, she's always been that way, except when she was young herself. The woman died of a stroke just like the Drohobycz husband. She was scrubbing a wall."

Lars was quiet: it was as if the foreign ape had calmed itself, and was now swinging tranquilly in his breast. He was relieved. He sank down under her flow. Did he believe any of it? It made him think of Heidi's fence, Heidi with her arms flung out just this way, insisting and insisting.

"That box"—her arms passed over his quilt, over the twisted papers—"well, it's gone. Lost. I looked everywhere for it. In every closet and cabinet of that flat. The husband let me look, he didn't care. He was in a hurry to get rid of every bit of it. That's how I found the pages in the shoes—looking for the box."

And went on, then, with the cadence of it, the mad consecutive-
ness: how the box was carried to Warsaw by the people who had
bought the woman's house, how when they showed her the box
she was outraged—it was money they wanted. Why should I pay
you? she said. For what? It can't be worth two zlotys. She told
them it wasn't a will in there, it was nothing at all, no one could
figure out what it was. The husband looked in the box and
shifted the papers and sniffed the dampness and said, No, it
isn't a will, it isn't a legacy, nothing like that. It's Jew-prayers,
what the Żydki pray, it's hexes and curses. So it turned out that
the people who had bought the house were glad to go all the way
back to Drohobycz without getting paid for the box, at least they
were safe from the hexes, and the woman said to her husband,
How do you know it's what the Żydki pray? Mother of God, he
said, I tried to read it, it's all a jumble, it's the way they pray.
And also the letters on the top, The Messiah, it's the Jews cursing
Our Lord. Get rid of it, the husband said. But it's good paper,
she said, thick and strong, I'll find some use for it, so after she
walked out in the rain one time, she stuffed some of the sheets
into her shoes. To keep the shape. And she told her lady, the
lady she worked for, whose husband was Tosiek Glowko, my
mother's special friend, a Party official, high up in the Party, she
told the lady that back in her old house in Drohobycz there was
a box of prayers, what the Jews pray, buried under the floor in
the cellar, and the people who bought the house wanted to get
money out of her just for returning it; but she wasn't a fool, it
wasn't her box to begin with, it was only scribbles in there—
real prayers, even what the Jews pray, come in prayerbooks. The
lady said, Then maybe it's actually not prayers, and the woman
said, My husband thinks the same, he says what the Jews pray
is hexes and curses, and besides it's scribbled all over with Our
Lord's name, in mockery. The lady recounted all this to her husband, Tosiek Glowko, my mother's special friend—she was laughing at these mysterious papers her maid was keeping in a funny

box dug up out of the ground. It's how they behave out there in those country towns, outlanders, hicks, they don't understand the world; the woman had this box for years in the cellar of her shack in Drohobycz, ever since the middle of the war; it's something the Jews left. Tosiek Glowko said, Drohobycz? Because he knew that was where my mother grew up, my mother grew up in Drohobycz and went to school there. But for my mother it wasn't a hick town, in her eyes it was a little Vienna. And then the woman scrubbed the kitchen wall, and Tosiek Glowko said to my mother, Oh my poor wife, her maid dropped dead right at her feet, she had a stroke in my poor wife's kitchen, we had to call the police—and do you know, this old woman is from your own town, she's from Drohobycz?

"You see," she finished, "that's how it went." She reached out over the quilt to gather in his father's strewn and confounded words. He watched her pile up the sheets and pat them and tap them, until she had constructed a neat rectangular stack. It struck Lars that there was an idiocy in this sudden tidying-up: he almost laughed. It was as if the order of the pages didn't matter to her in the least. The progenitrix of chaos. She stared across at him. "*Now* do you see how it went? My mother heard about the manuscript—"

"From her lover. The man high up in the Party."

"—and I got on the bus and rode across Warsaw and found the old man and took away all the papers there were."

"He let you? The woman's husband? The widower," he corrected.

"Well, there he was, running around and collecting whatever he could put his hands on, wherever his wife had stuck them. In the oven, can you imagine? Three sheets in the oven. And six in those shoes. He let me look everywhere. By then there wasn't any box. The box was gone."

"But why you?" Lars urged. "Why would he give them to you?"

"He would have given them to anyone. He would have burned them in the trash. I got there in time to save them from the trash. He was afraid." She sent out a pale little smile, perilously edged. "He thought she'd died from the curse, don't you see? Because the curse had been dug up. Because when he told her to get rid of the papers she didn't obey."

It came to him then that he didn't believe a word. What an invention! The best inventions are those with the most substantial particulars. A fabricator. Or else a cunning inheritor, a spinner of old fables: buried vessels, spells, incantations, magical instant dyings. Or else simply crazed. Adela! This name of terror lifted straight out of his father's spectral scenery. *I could not tell whether these pictures were implanted in my mind by Adela's tales or whether I had witnessed them myself. . . . Perhaps in our treachery there was secret approval of the victorious Adela to whom we dimly ascribed some commission and assignment from forces of a higher order. . . . Adela, warm from sleep and with unkempt hair, was grinding coffee in a mill which she pressed to her white bosom, imparting her warmth to the broken beans.*

Crazed. A grinder of broken beans.

He accused, "You've mixed up all the pages."

"It makes no difference. You can shuffle them however you like. It has the same effect no matter what. You'll see for yourself when you begin."

"Begin what? I'm not beginning anything." He asked, "Why do you call yourself Adela?"

"It's my name."

"It's from *Cinnamon Shops*. From *Sanatorium*. Is that why you took it?"

"I didn't take it. People don't give themselves their own names, do they? My father picked it. He told my mother to call me Adela. This was before I was born, when they knew she was pregnant. Then he was shot in the wild action, you've heard of the wild action? My mother ran to Brazil, she got out, even then. She could do it, she's crafty that way. Even then."

An electric jolt: the ape was hurled. "Your father—" Lars stood in his little space, between the table and the bed. The light was still brilliant, a great unholy glare: her head against it looked inky-dark. He could not see her eyes with the morning's brilliance in his own. "It's only a story," he said. He did not say: Your mother's a cloud, your father's a fog. "Don't go spreading such a thing—you'll only do yourself damage. It isn't possible. A figment. A lie."

"Mrs. Eklund *said* you'd carry on." But she faltered—he saw what her trouble was. There was a word and she was refusing it. She was resisting. "She said you'd act as if, as if—" She plucked up the white beret and came to stand with her face close to his. "As if you owned every syllable. Every syllable he ever put down."

The breath of her voice steamed into his nostrils. Her voice was hot. How free she seemed, how like a bedouin!

"If that old fellow in Warsaw let you take away the manuscript—just like that—"

"Priest," Adela threw out. "*That's* what she said. You act like a priest!"

"—then the other version isn't so."

"There isn't any other version. It's only what I've told you."

"Mrs. Eklund's version. The one she got from you—that *The Messiah* was waiting for you to come and pick it up. There it was, in Warsaw. In Drohobycz. Under the ground. Under the arm of the man with the coat. God knows where it was! Loitering there—decades—waiting for you to turn up, all the way from Brazil! It was being *saved*, that's the point. For the daughter." He wanted to be raucous, he wanted to jeer; instead he found himself raveled in a simple-minded knot of a cough. "The daughter! They were keeping it for you."

"They weren't. It wasn't being saved."

"No one else could have gotten hold of it. Only the daughter."
He ended, "That's Mrs. Eklund's version."

"I never told her any of that."

"You never told her you're the daughter—"

"I did. I am." She gave him a look of fire. "A priest is just what's needed. You'd be on your knees, wouldn't you? On your knees to every word. You'd think you were anointed."

"There can't be a daughter," Lars said.

"You won't do it. I can see that. You won't. You're exactly the one to do it, but you won't."

"Mrs. Eklund's going to introduce you to her Polish Princess, wait and see. The Princess translates a thousand times better than I can. Ask Mrs. Eklund." He was perfectly serene: he was certain that the ape, exhausted at last, had foolishly dropped off. He said, "There's no logic in the daughter business, is there? You can't make it come out right. It won't come out."

She fixed him, eye to eye. Two vertical trenches like his own. "He was my mother's art teacher. In the high school in Droho-bycz. She was fifteen years old. She modeled for his drawings."

His drawings! A mistake, a mistake!

Those photographs. Heidi had misled him. Or else he had misled Heidi. They had misled each other. They had misconceived. They had not known how to imagine. The photographs had arrested them; had *held* them. The photographs had held their heads like a pincers! Their heads, pinched together, side by side, peering into the faces in the circle of women. Always the circle of women. He, the author of *The Messiah*, the only male; the central figure; ringed round by women. Heidi testing those faces, scrutinizing, reconnoitering: together they had fallen into the eyes and mouths of these women. Not one of them was the lover. Not one. They had never thought of a child. They had never imagined a pupil. One of his pupils!

Adela said, "He used to take her home. He invented different costumes for her. He asked her to pose, to playact. You can see yourself if you want. You can look her up."

"Look her up?"

"In the illustrations. She's there in most of them. A little man in a top hat, with a giant dog. A boy with big buttons. A fellow in riding boots. A woman in high heels wearing a coat with a fur collar. All of those. Sometimes she's naked."

A pupil. The high school. Smeared with provincial paste and paint. The drawings! That triangular little jaw, those unearthly eyes, those tapered small torsos; dwindling little feet and toes. A child!

"The pregnancy frightened him," she announced.

"Where are you going? You can't—" He took desolate note of it: she was packing up. "Stop it, what are you doing? You haven't let me see—" Now she was shoving the stack of papers—creased and assaulted—back into the white plastic bag.

"She loved him more than he loved her. He was afraid to be connected to anyone. In the end," she flung back, "there was the wild action, so it didn't matter."

A stride like a pounce. Another; she was at the door.

"Don't take it away. You haven't let me have a look. I haven't *seen* it. Wait!" he pleaded. "I haven't told you *my* side."

"I know your side. You don't care. If you cared you would do it, you would work at putting it in the world."

"No, no, it's something else. Mrs. Eklund didn't tell you—"

"I've contradicted something she said? All right, then you've shown me what you think. You think she can't be relied on."

"I haven't shown you anything. You don't know anything."

He tore at her like a drunkard and snatched the bag from her grip.

"Give that back."

"It's mine," he said.

"Give it back."

"He's my father. I'm his son!"

The foetal ape was awake, unfurled, raging; huge. *The Messiah* was light, light; it was not heavy at all. Lars drew it against him, he bunched it against his chest: the exulting, the ape, the heaving, the hurling!

"Give it *back*."

She ground toward him, she was fit and fleet—she twisted the plastic bag to pry it free of him. They crushed the papers between them: her tongue snapped, he drove off the hole of her turbulent mouth—she spat. He thought of her poor crumpled breasts. He was steady now, *The Messiah* was in his arms, he would not let her take it away. Her spittle was on his cheek. He raised one leg—the leg was heavy, it had a weight—and kicked Adela to the floor.

He saw her head near his victorious shoes; her hands were on her breasts. He was a colossus staring down.

"There's only me. There isn't any son. You're a schemer, you're a thief. You'll say anything."

How distant and small, how Lilliputian, this fury of hers! Her head, far below, a dead bird. Then in a sudden spiraling of pure flight, as elastic as the rising up of a bird, she jumped her haunches into a squat and flew up to beat at the white bag—it slipped from him, she had it in her fist; and escaped. Escaped.

A mistake, a mistake! She was gone, she was away. The door vibrated on its hinges. Violence like a burning; the door still rocking. Or else it was his bones in their long shiver. The broken beans of his shaking. How he had crushed her breasts, how he had crumpled his father's brain. That cradling of *The Messiah*: good God, hadn't he held it in his arms? It had possessed, for one holy hour, his house; his bed; his quilt. He ought to have been on his knees to it; she had warned him. He might have knelt there—gazing—before the caves and grottoes of his quilt.

And not one word taken. Not one word. Not a glimpse. He

had been as near to it as to the apparition of his father's eye. *The Messiah* in his arms, and lost again!

He ran through the passage and outdoors to the sidewalk; she was not there. The pavement was empty. She was nowhere in the street. Whatever direction he looked—he whirled and whirled in the cold air—she was not there. She had turned a corner; she was out of sight. He knew nothing about her: only that he had made her his prey, because of *The Messiah*. A snatch of panic no bigger than a ragged inch caught him then: it seemed to him Adela was a churning angel. The white bag was flying beside her into the niche behind the wall. Beguiled, he watched her set it down on the leather chair with the cracked leg; she was delivering *The Messiah*. She left it there for him and vanished. He understood it was the business of angels to vanish.

When he put his head into the angle of the little secret hallway, the leather chair was in its place, with nothing on it but the diurnal dust.

11

IT WAS STILL only noon. The bright perished day hung
before him. He walked out to the clamor of the *Morgontörn*,
where the secretaries were eating sandwiches of cold meat and
boiled egg. In the book department the stewpot had not yet
gathered. Lars plucked up a volume, medium-thick, from the
piles of review copies stacked against the baseboards. A neat small
black mouse-pellet was lodged in the binding, so he put it down
again and chose another. This turned out to be much thicker.
It was the newest novel by the prolific Ann-Charlott Almgren, a
name he knew—it was considerably celebrated—though he had
never read her, not even her famous *Nytt och Gammalt*. He
inserted his thumb between the pages somewhere among the
middle chapters to catch the smell of the thing. It promised to
touch on lust, deceit, ambition, and death, and looked good
enough for his purpose.

He had a purpose. Gunnar's cubicle was vacant; so was
Anders's. He decided on Gunnar's and commenced. The novel
was called *Illusion*. He admired the plot, which was founded
on the principle of ambush. A kind and modest elderly spinster
—a self-taught painter—falls in love with a ne'er-do-well, a

beautiful and clever young man. She has declined to show her paintings because she believes them to be of no merit. The young man is the first to see them; she has never had the courage to reveal them to anyone before. But the young man recognizes at once that she is a hidden genius. He agrees to marry her if she will consent to a deception: he will claim the paintings as his own and give them to the world. The scheme is a grand success; the marriage is happy. The seeming painter is taken up by the fashionable and honored everywhere. But by then the new husband, awash in charm and glory, has attached himself to a seductive young woman, the very art critic whose lavish commendations have elevated his reputation. The self-effacing elderly wife, discovering the liaison . . . et cetera, et cetera. The book weighed in Lars's hands; it weighed him down. It was as heavy as loss. (And *The Messiah* in his arms—light, ah how light!)

An hour and a half to read. Finished. Half an hour more: his review over and done with. ("Composed." Spat out.) Another hour: bungling and bumbling on Gunnar's hostile machine. Painful, a plunge into needles. Then it was three o'clock. The stewpot was beginning to straggle in with its perilous shards of laughter; but Lars knocked on Nilsson's office door and offered to wait—he stood there mute and patient—while Nilsson looked over his pages.

"Well, well, well," Nilsson said. "What do you think of that? My my my. Very nice. This is very nice, Lars. It's something new for you." And he said: "You're going to work out. I always knew you would. I've always had confidence in you, Lars. Not that I haven't felt alone in it, believe me. But it wouldn't surprise me a bit if you started giving Friday a run for its money, what do you think of that?" And he said: "Keep it up, Lars. Give me two months of this kind of work and I'll get you your own cubicle, how about it?" And he said: "Just don't relapse. No more Broch, no more Canetti; a little Kundera goes a long way. I imagine you had to get Central Europe out of your system—I told them you'd shuck it off in the end." And he said: "Lars, listen! You're going to work out."

Lars sidled around the margins of the stewpot—it never noticed him at all—and gravitated toward home and bed. "Those crocodiles," he thought he heard Nilsson say. Or was it "Those cormorants"? Impossible to tell from such a distance—Lars was under his quilt. Over which, lightly—lightly and aloft!—*The Messiah* had skimmed. His eyes leaked, his nostrils were in commotion. A convulsion of fatigue. Yesterday's missing nap; the migrations of displaced sleep. A mesmerizing cloud. He slept, in order to wake to his father's eye.

When he woke there was only absence. Nothing formed in the black air. The empty dark sent out nothing at all. The greased beak did not seize him. The alabaster egg did not materialize. Lars threw off the quilt and stared as if his own eyeballs were two breathing bellows inflated by the bottommost power of his pumping lungs. His head was filled with the battering, plodding, butting force of that staring, that bulging. But the visitation did not occur. No sphere appeared. The author of *The Messiah* had withdrawn. Lars's father's eye did not return.

It was seven o'clock. He had not eaten all day long, as if he had deliberately undertaken a fast. But it was only because he had forgotten hunger. After defeat in battle men do not remember food. He tied on his scarf and squashed his cap over his ears. On the floor near his bed, a white patch. He bent to it, and, bending, grieved over the afterimage of Adela's hair bundled like feathers at his feet. Dead bird. He had kicked her down: his father's daughter. His sister, his sister. He saw then that the white patch was a page of *The Messiah*, overlooked in the battle and left behind. He snatched it up with the knowledge that his right hand would burst like a grenade at the touch of the sheet.

He was ready to lose his right hand for the sake of an errant paragraph out of *The Messiah*.

The patch was not that. He picked it up: Adela's white beret. It was not what he wanted, so he tossed it on his bed and fell into the night toward Heidi's shop.

12

THE SHOP was shut up and black. But a yellow mist spread forward from the back room: the lit daffodil; she was there. His boots were wet and stuck all over with grit. A matchstick had caught in the left sole. Lars began by habit to pull them off—then he thought better of it. It wasn't his intention to please Heidi. Every evening after hours she ordered the Turkish boy to mop up; the Turkish boy wasn't allowed to go home until the mud of the day's customers had been washed away. Lars stamped his feet in the vestibule. Instantly he stopped stamping. He wasn't a visitor, he wasn't anyone's guest. He had the right of entry—he had it in his pocket. The borrowed cold key. It went into the lock.

"Who's there? What's that?" A raw dark voice. The smell of something roasting. "Is it that woman? It's that woman?"

"It can't be. There wasn't any knock. I told her she'd have to knock. The door's locked." This was Heidi, calling from behind the fence of books. She shuffled out; she had her slippers on.

"Then who is it? Why isn't it that woman, if she's coming? We're closed, can't they tell that?"

Lars said, "Mrs. Eklund—"

The raw dark fidgety voice, an actor's voice: "It's not that woman, it's a man. Didn't you close up for the night?"

"Never mind, it's only Lars. He's brought your key back, now you'll have your extra. Lars," Heidi said, "let me introduce you. Here is Dr. Olle Eklund. And here is Lars Andemening. Now you see how proper we all are. Dr. Eklund is always so fond of the forms."

A very large man was sitting at Heidi's little table with an almost empty teacup in front of him, smoking a pipe. He looked like an oversized sleek startled horse, with long nostrils punched into a scanty lump of cartilage, a long face, and a long tumescent head, bald and bright. His eyeglasses splashed light. The crown of his head seemed polished. He was fastidiously dressed, in a coat and vest with glinting silver buttons. He wore a silver ring on the third finger of each hand, and there was something about the buttons and the rings, and also in the way he shot out his big fingers toward Lars, that suggested a sea captain. Or else it was his seaweedy merman's odor, mixed with the meatlike scorch of tobacco, strong and salty. His chin was well-shaved, without a visible prickle; it had a shine of its own.

Lars took the man's hand—how hot it was—and shook it. "Is it Dr. Eklund?" he said.

"Dr. Eklund got back early this morning," Heidi said. "Such a strain, such a tiring day after his trip—"

Lars examined the man. He watched him lift his cup and put it down. He watched him light a match and draw on his pipe. "I was here myself this morning," he said.

"My little Turk *told* me you came by—he doesn't like you, why is that? I was over at the flat, filling the refrigerator. It's different with two at home." Heidi scraped a chair out of the shadows. "Sit down, you brute, and tell us about it. You knocked her down, didn't you? I've neglected to notice that side of you— that poor Adela! She ran howling back here to complain I'd sent her to a thug."

Lars said, *"Is it Dr. Eklund?"*

Dr. Eklund held out his cup. "A little more."

Heidi bustled to the kettle. "She's coming tonight. To consult Dr. Eklund. If he weren't Dr. Eklund"—Lars saw she was going to be whimsical—"she couldn't consult him, *nicht wahr?"*

"She's not even bruised! Is she bruised?"

"For heaven's sake, this isn't a health clinic, what do you think we are? She's coming about what's in that bag. I promised her this time no one would knock her down. I don't imagine she'll be glad to see you, Lars. You'd better leave before."

"I don't understand how he got in," Dr. Eklund said.

"With your key. I gave him your key."

"If he knocks people down you shouldn't give him my key."

"I thought," Lars said heavily, "there wasn't any Dr. Eklund."

"Lars believes in ghosts," Heidi explained.

"You made me think he was made up."

"Cogito, ergo sum," Dr. Eklund said. "Why would you think a thing like that?"

"Not everyone has to exist."

"That is remarkably plausible."

"He means he's an orphan," Heidi said. "He was one of those refugee orphans. He doesn't know who his mother is."

"I don't know who my father is either," Lars said.

"Here's something new!" Heidi cried. "Your father is the author of *Cinnamon Shops*. Your father is the author of *Sanatorium*. Your father is the author of *The Messiah*. That's who your father is." She let out her rapid doglike laugh.

"I don't have a father."

"You've lost your father? But not his eye," she taunted. "You've kept that eye?"

"It's gone. It's not there."

Dr. Eklund asked, "Eye? Eye? Where is such an eye?"

"An intelligent boy, but subject to hallucinations," Heidi declaimed—did she mean to humiliate him? A wave of regret.

He had entrusted her with his arcane mote: his visitation, his apparition. There was no eye. It had left him. It would not come back again.

"Hardly a boy. If he grew whiskers he'd be a graybeard," Dr. Eklund said through his pipe.

Lars in his shame felt himself stumbling over a certain familiarity of inflection, of accent. Sibilance. Something was too accustomed here; he could not assess it. A strangeness in Dr. Eklund's voice. Strange because not strange enough.

"A slight resemblance nevertheless," Dr. Eklund continued. "A very minor resemblance. The chin, perhaps. No more than an inkling, yes? The summer of 1938—I'm not mistaken about this—I saw him drinking tea—steaming tea—at a café in a little outdoor courtyard. In Paris this was. He was pointed out to me. Then I absolutely recognized him for myself."

"Dr. Eklund is fluent in Polish," Heidi supplied.

"There was very much Polish being spoken at that table. A group of three or four. They had been to the galleries. The subject was art. I remember what a hot day it was, and still that fellow was drinking steaming tea! No different from what's in this cup. Hotter, probably. Sometimes one or two of them would retreat back into French, but mainly it was Polish. Though *that* fellow never said a word. He looked like a hayseed, he wore his pants cuffs too high. You could see an inch more of sock than was decent—imagine, this was only a couple of years or so after *Cinnamon Shops*. A piece of luck."

It seemed a muddle—who exactly was it Dr. Eklund was saying he had seen in Paris? Then it occurred to Lars what it was he was hearing in Dr. Eklund's throat. He had thought at first it might have been the muffling of the pipe. But it was not the pipe. Dr. Eklund's vowels—was it possible?—were not unlike Adela's. Dr. Eklund—was it possible?—was not a Swede at all.

"You never mentioned it," Lars accused. "About the Polish."

"Dr. Eklund doesn't like it known. He gets people *out*, you

see. He does his best. He's always done his best. He got Mrs.
Rozanowska out, for instance."

"He got the Princess out?"

"That was a long time ago—you've heard all about that.
Together with her husband. Dr. Eklund got them out and then
he got them *in*. For all you know," she said maliciously, "he got
you out. In your swaddling clothes! He knows how to do those
tricks, don't you, Olle?"

Dr. Eklund took a discreet sip. "I don't like it when you
give things away."

"You've got your key back."

"Not everything given away is recoverable."

How theatrical they were, Dr. and Mrs. Eklund! Two old
troupers in rehearsal. Lars leaned his chair toward Dr. Eklund
and bathed his whole head in the roast-meat cloud that was
seeping out of Dr. Eklund's pipe. "Who was it you saw," he
said, "in Paris?"

"That fellow. That author of yours."

"In Paris? You saw him in Paris?"

"Only for a few moments. A piece of luck."

"But you *saw* him! You saw his face?"

"He had a pointed chin. I remember that."

"And what else? How did he look?"

"Like someone drinking hot tea in July."

Lars turned on Heidi: "Your husband *saw* him! You never
mentioned it, you never told—"

"I'm hearing it now for the first time myself."

"In a pig's foot you are. And on top of that the Polish! To
have a husband *fluent in Polish*," he echoed, "and never to say
a word about it—"

"Well, you should have figured that out on your own."

"Figured it out!" How preposterous she was; how senseless,
how operatic. "Why not send Adela to your husband, if it's translation she wants? *I'm* not the one she's looking for!"

"Dr. Eklund prefers not to translate. Dr. Eklund is obliged to go back and forth. He follows things up. He gets things out."

"Translation is not my interest," Dr. Eklund affirmed. "Especially of dubious manuscripts."

"What a baby you are, Lars. Naïve. It's not only ghosts you believe in. It's a question of detective work, can't you understand that? Agents. Connections. Combinations. How else would I have gotten hold of those Warsaw items? Who am I to get hold of such things? A little hole-in-the-wall bookseller—"

"I don't like it," Dr. Eklund said again, "when you give things away."

Heidi swept on. "You think a letter dated 1934 grows on trees? You think pieces of a memoir about a dinner conversation in Warsaw in 1936 can be picked up in the street? Just like that? Lars, please, let me ask you—left to yourself, what would you have come up with? Left to yourself, that's the point! I'll tell you what—you would have come up with the only scrap you *did* come up with! An American review from the *Morgontörn*'s trash barrel, that's what." The black eyebrows were wobbling like rocking-horse manes. "No, no, it's not so simple. You dreamers would like it to be simple, you would like everything to turn on the issue of literary passion. I suppose Warsaw releases its valuables just like that? Or maybe it's only a matter of telephoning long-distance to a dealer in Drohobycz, ha! You're a baby, you don't understand the world. You think the world is made of literature. You think reality is a piece of paper."

What was it she was telling him? It was something to do with Dr. Eklund. Somehow it was about Dr. Eklund—which couldn't be, in any case, his right name. Dr. Eklund wasn't a Swede. Was he even a doctor? Was he, with his weedy pungencies, a sea captain in earnest? He got things out—people and things. He got things in—things and people. A smoother of obstinacies. When Dr. Eklund was said to be in Copenhagen, or on his hospital rounds, or asleep in the flat, did it mean he was actually in Budapest? Had he really—four years after the publication of *Cinnamon Shops*, in a summertime Paris already darkening toward war—had he really seen Lars's father?

Lars had no father. No father ever again. He was giving his father up—to the probabilities, if not to the facts. There were no facts. Beyond the shooting there was nothing at all. Only the turbulence of desire, the merciless boil of a saving chimerical eye. The eye of deliverance. Of redemption. It had burst out over the little cave of Lars's quilt like the wheel of a sun. A fiery hoop. A roaring egg. An intelligence. A devouring certainty. Gone; erased; wiped out. Heidi didn't appear to be at all unsettled by these whirlwind blanks: it didn't touch her that Lars had thrown off his claim to the author of *The Messiah*, that he was willing now to withdraw to nothingness, that he was no one's son, that he had no father; that he was undone. It didn't touch her, either way. She had never believed in his case; it didn't matter to her that he was tearing up his case then and there. It didn't seem to please her.

"I'm stopping, Mrs. Eklund," he said. "It's over. I'm quitting."

"What's over? What are you quitting?"

"I told you. I don't have a father."

"Did you ever have a father? I never thought you did."

"Adam, the father of us all," Dr. Eklund said.

"No more Warsaw items. No letters, no memoirs, no photographs, no drawings, no proverbs, no quotations—I won't be bothering you," Lars said.

"Not at all a bother," Dr. Eklund said. "More in the way of business."

"Dr. Eklund is always so much concerned with anything to do with the shop," Heidi said.

"My father has nothing to do with the shop."

"Your ex-father. Shouldn't you be saying your ex-father?"

"Take my word that I'm finished."

"Really finished?"

"It's the end."

"Oh, but *we* don't quit," she countered.

We? Who was "we"? It was, Lars considered, a new "we." Now it included Dr. Eklund.

"Dr. Eklund," she pointed out, "has had a certain interest in accumulating these items."

"These evidences," Dr. Eklund suggested.

"These evidences. That's why he agreed to see Adela. He's worn out—just look how worn out the poor man is. But he agreed to see her anyhow, and you know why?"

"Why?" asked Dr. Eklund. Raillery, or was he hurrying her on?

"Because he sympathizes. He knows how you're consumed by all this. He understands you, Lars."

"Comprehends. Penetrates," Dr. Eklund offered. "The attraction—the seduction, the magnetism—of a sublime text. This is a feeling I myself admit to."

"Dr. Eklund is so to speak your psychological twin."

"Now don't go too far," Dr. Eklund said. "I don't propose to be in this gentleman's category. There's no one else just like him. Not in Stockholm, no."

"My category? What category is that?"

"*U*sefulness," Heidi said, covering it over with her joking little bark.

A single wild church bell. If not a church bell, then a kind of gong.

"Good God, what *is* it?" Heidi burst out. "I told her just to knock—did she break the glass? She broke it!"

Dr. Eklund sprang up—he wasn't at all tired; he was robust and acrobatic, more of a sea captain than ever—and sprinted across the length of the shop to the door, darting in and out of the blocks of shelves like an oversized rat in a tunnel.

Heidi reached up to switch on the lights; the shop looked suddenly open for business.

"You nearly broke my glass!"

"Well, but I didn't." Adela rubbed her foot in the slide-marks across the vestibule. "I slipped in the snow with this thing. Right against the door. It's started coming down again."

"Look at your shoes," Heidi said. "You'll leak all over my floors. The boy mopped only an hour ago."

Adela was bareheaded; Lars knew why. Her hair was sprinkled with snow-beads. She was not carrying the white plastic bag. Her arms were pressed around the belly of a round brass jug; a sort of amphora. It was either a very large flower vase or a very modest umbrella stand. The open mouth of it had been shielded from the weather by a plastic shower cap.

"No hat? In the snow you should wear a hat," Dr. Eklund reprimanded. It was, Lars noted, a version of Heidi's whimsicality; it was part of his being histrionic. And what if this woman clutching a barrel, or an urn, or whatever it was, did or didn't wear a hat? Dr. Eklund was too suddenly intimate; he was ready instantly to absorb her. There was a clownish anxiety in it. He was looking her over like a potential deckhand signing on for a voyage. He wasn't sure she would do. He was ready to order, advise, interrogate.

Lars said, "I've got her hat in my house."

Adela turned; Lars watched the startled tide rise in her face.

"It's in my bed. Your hat."

"You! This man, this insane man! It's enough for one day! Why should he *be* here? Who asked him to come?" The two vertical trenches drew together like a pair of fence pickets. But it was more calculation than rage.

"No one asked him. He just turned up," Heidi said.

"Because he had my key," Dr. Eklund complained. "He took my key, that's why."

Adela clashed the brass amphora down on the little back-room table, an inch from Dr. Eklund's cup. "He'll say anything. He'll do anything. The right thing would be to call the police."

"Now that would be the wrong thing," Dr. Eklund said.

"The police are for thieves, aren't they?"

"Now, now. Hold on, please. A manuscript of dubious origin. We don't yet know whether it is or it isn't *The Messiah*."

"That's exactly the question Dr. Eklund's going to settle," Heidi said placatingly. It was as if she was being launched—was it by invisible confluences, was it by Dr. Eklund himself, was it really by the thought of the police?—on a peacekeeping mission. "You don't have to worry about Lars. He's had a crisis and it's done with."

Adela blew out a ferocious breath. "An assault! Oh yes, done with—I told him everything and he knocked me down."

"Because you weren't letting me have a look."

"A look?" said Dr. Eklund. "A look at what?"

"*The Messiah*. She ran off with it in that bag."

"He tried to steal it."

"You should have let him have a look," Dr. Eklund said severely.

"You should have let him," Heidi said. "It wasn't fair. Anyhow he'll apologize, you'll see. Lars, you'll apologize, won't you?"

"Never *mind*," Dr. Eklund muttered; the whimsicality was drained out. "It gets late for our business. If she doesn't want him, he should go away."

Lars said, "Where's that bag? You don't have that bag with you."

"I don't have my hat," Adela mocked.

"Why doesn't he *go*?" Dr. Eklund said, fidgeting with another match.

It was remarkable: Dr. Eklund's voice—the habit of emphasis, the hard little undulation in *go*—was exactly Adela's. The sea captain and Adela were from some far part of the world —the same part. The same modulations, the same eruptions and lavalike descent of the vowels. It was clear they had once been neighbors, Dr. Eklund and Adela. And yet Adela was somehow a provocation. Dr. Eklund the sympathizer, Dr. Eklund the psychological twin—now here was Dr. Eklund trying to throw Lars out. The change had arrived with Adela. It was as if a warning vibration had been set off, some sudden machine or subtle alarm Lars could detect the hum of—in the background, behind the shelves, out of sight.

It made Heidi his unexpected advocate. "He has the right to stay, why shouldn't he stay?" She was accommodatingly soft, she was amiable, she was all at once mollifying; she meant to take his part. "He cares about what's in that manuscript more than anyone alive. It's his *mania*," she said, naming it like an awful contagion. "It's what he concentrates on. I can't claim he's ever knocked me down to get at it. Not actually, not in my bones. But talk of assault! I'm the one who can testify to that! He's gone after my brain, and isn't that worse? He's made me pick at all his leavings. I've had to chew over whatever he's chewed. Such people get born, God knows how or to whom, to compensate for what isn't there. They pour the strangest things into the void. Like sand into a sack."

Mild babble: she kept on with it. She said she had become his slave, he had enslaved her to his concentration, to his obsession. His mind was no better than any other single-product manufacturing contraption. He had fettered her to it, he had fettered himself, and at the same time he was uncontrollable, he couldn't be restrained. He was one of the century's casualties, in his own way a victim. He took on everyone's loss; everyone's foolish grief. Foolish because unstinting. Rescue was the only thought he kept in his head—he was arrogant about it, he was steady, he wanted to salvage every scrap of paper all over Europe. Europe's savior! His head was full of Europe—all those obscure languages in all those shadowy places where there had been all those shootings—in the streets, in the forests. He had attached himself to the leavings of tyranny, tragedy, confusion.

"There's no one else like him," she finished. "Not anywhere. It's just what Dr. Eklund says—a category of his own."

Through all this Adela was flaunting a crooked caustic smile. "All right, a madman. You called him priest and you meant madman. Then why on earth would you send me to him? You sent me there!"

Heidi twisted her stout little torso. "You wanted a translator."

"You knew he wouldn't do it. And you sent me!"

"Well, I thought he should have a look."

"The priest should have a look? Or the savior should? Or just the madman? Mrs. Eklund, he never *considered* translating. You knew that. Don't tell me you didn't! *That's* why I didn't let him have a look."

"No, no," Heidi protested, "you're not following. The way he went after Polish—didn't I see for myself how he went after Polish? He swallowed it right down. He's after what's primary—"

"He tells stupendous lies."

"What he wants is the original of things. It's what I said, it's just what I told you. He's a priest of the original—isn't that what I told you?"

She was his advocate, she was taking his part. It was a sort of play. He was in a theater. Lars felt himself shut out. Behind a curtained proscenium—but the curtain was sealed against him—some unintelligible drama raged. Even as onlooker he had no rational place in it. What was he to be henceforth, if he was not to be his father's son? And she, the daughter, this falsehood of a daughter? The author of *The Messiah* was nobody's father now. What Lars had given up! A capitulation; he had surrendered to the false daughter's tale. He had no solid tale of his own to set against it; only this rush of blood. Hers was as probable as anything else in the wilderness of Europe forty years ago. These stories had their plausibility. Lars had—what did he have? His old certainty, grown out of him like a fingernail.

He chopped it off. He stood there stripped of verisimilitude. Was she nobody's daughter? Then he, so much the more, was nobody's son.

How hard it was to breathe, to breathe in and out, without illumination! Everything quenched, snuffed, suffocated. Surrendered. The light that rode forth like a horn, as though a huge saddle had been flung over the flanks of the universe, a saddle with its fiery horn of light, riding out from his father's fixed eye . . . Dissolved. It had let itself die. It would not return.

The smell of roasting flame: Dr. Eklund striking still another match—match after match—to rekindle his smothered pipe.

The women went on contending. It was a quarrel; it was not a quarrel. It might have been the pretense of a quarrel. Marionettes. Heidi's back room rife with plots, cabals—why was he thinking that? A stage frenzy: willed, directed, cued. Adela wanted him to go. Heidi wanted him to stay.

Dr. Eklund was indifferent. "Let the fellow go, let the fellow stay. If the text is valid—that's the proper question."

Adela said bitterly, "He thinks it belongs to him."

"Now, now," Dr. Eklund said.

"He takes things. You heard him! He's got my hat."

Their two voices were just the same. A family sound. The smoky air had becalmed itself. Nothing spontaneous rose in that space. Dr. Eklund propped his lit pipe on his saucer. Then he pushed cup, saucer, and pipe aside. The brass amphora—it had no handles; it was no more than a dented old pot—stretched its archaic shape up from the middle of the little table. From the pocket of his vest Dr. Eklund drew out, by its big black stem, a large round magnifying glass and placed it next to cup, saucer, and pipe.

"Smart!" Heidi said, tapping her knuckles against the pot, making it ring. "To think of bringing that. With the snow coming down."

"So. The Solomonic moment. Then let us examine our dubious author."

With both hands Dr. Eklund took hold of the brass amphora and raised it above the table. There it was, high up, traveling at a decent steady speed—a torpedo; a whale with its mouth wide; a chalice. Midway he tipped it over, until the mouth hung upside down, vomiting disorder, chaos: a shower of ragged white wings, a jumbled armada of white sails. A hundred sheets spiraled out—crumpled, splotched, speckled, aged. What had littered Lars's quilt that morning came tumbling now out of Ali Baba's jar.

"Smart!" Heidi said again. "Keeping everything dry!"

Dr. Eklund clanged down the emptied-out amphora. It hit the floor with the reverberating note of a cymbal, and rolled on its side toward Dr. Eklund's feet. It was plain that Dr. Eklund —sorcery!—had instantly understood what to do with this peculiar vessel. He had seen that it was there to be turned upside down and emptied out.

Lars looked over at Adela. She had moved to crouch beside Dr. Eklund—she was picking up the runaway sheets that had fallen to the floor. She was picking them up and putting them on the table, with the others. That wounded handwriting— buried, beaten, bruised, drowned. She lifted each stray page, one by one. She had carried them to Heidi's shop in that tall metal trophy-cup: Hebe the cupbearer, messenger, deliverer. He knew her as nothing else. He wanted to cry, Ulrika, Birgitta! Not one but two wives! And a child, lost, stolen! Himself now without even that paintbox. The last trace expunged. Erased. And Adela? Had she had a life prior to bags and jars? A woman his own age, graying like himself. She was not his sister; he had no sister, he had no father, he had no inkling of his mother's name. He had named himself, in secret: Lazarus Baruch. Who was to tell him otherwise, who was to deny him these twinings

and entanglings? And, through dictionary divinations and caba-
listic displacements: Lars Andemening. Who was there to pre-
vent it? He had an orphan's terrifying freedom to choose. He
could become whatever he wished; no one could prohibit it, he
could choose his own history. He could choose and he could
relinquish. He was horribly, horribly free.

And she? Adela? Was there a husband behind the scenes?
Had she left a trail of some kind? Did she have a child? A
father?

Dr. Eklund did not hurry. His magnifying glass hovered
pitilessly. He seemed to be studying one word at a time; or else
one letter of one word. Again he burrowed inside his vest pocket.
A document inside an envelope. He was comparing the inky
loops of the document with the inky loops—broken, beaten,
hidden—that had flown out of the brass amphora.

"It recurs," Dr. Eklund said. "Observe how it recurs. The
telltale spur. This omnipresent hook. A shepherd's crook. Or a
bishop's."

"Dr. Eklund," Heidi said, "is a holographic authority. A
world authority. People summon him for verification from all
over. He goes all over Europe. He's been to South America. They
call on him everywhere."

Dr. Eklund reached for his pipe, inserted it between his lips,
and sucked. "Soon we will strike," he said, "on the truth."

A wail came loose in Lars. The foetal ape that lived alongside his inmost belly-organs snapped itself alert; it lurched. "The
truth!" he said. "Malice, it's malice! With a schoolgirl, his own
pupil! As if such a man—*such* a man—would copulate with a
child!"

Dr. Eklund began a scanty fragment of hum. Heidi took off
her slippers and put them side by side under the daffodil and
slid onto her cot: her face had thickened; her lids had thickened.
"You should wait for the verdict," she murmured.

"There isn't any verdict. There's only what's really there," Adela said from the floor.

The magnifying glass hovered; wandered left, wandered right. Dr. Eklund continued to hum—two bars and silence; three bars and silence. The bits of it suggested something between a lullaby and a sea chanty; it made Lars dimly restive, skittish. His little fear—he remembered it. It was trickling back, old, unaccountable, recognizable. And here was Dr. Eklund provoking it, pricking it alive again: Dr. Eklund with his pirate's fingers and their glittering rings, pinching page after page of the lost *Messiah*, and the great lens circling.

"No question. No question at all," Dr. Eklund pronounced. "Observe, observe. The capitals. As specifiable as a fingerprint. You won't find another *W* in the world like this fellow's. You won't find another *T*. What we have here"—he held the magnifier aloft, like a bishop's crook—"is entirely genuine. Authentic, I guarantee it. It is what it purports to be. I have no doubt of it. I would stake everything on it. The original."

Heidi, drowsy, the threads of her white bangs weaving like the smoke from Dr. Eklund's pipe, purred languidly from her cot: "A forgery. It could be a very good forgery. Olle, you know how clever a forger can be," and shut her eyes.

Adela sat like a doll, a foot away from the brass amphora, immobile, braced against the leg of the table. *Adela is fast asleep, her mouth half open, her face relaxed and absent; but her closed lids are transparent, and on their thin parchment the night is writing its pact with the devil, half text, half picture, full of erasures, corrections, and scribbles.*

"My good woman," Dr. Eklund urged, "no forger on earth can duplicate these shepherd's crooks. However expert. Not the most inspired master, believe me! Here is a letter, to a certain Tadeusz Breza, written by our author, and here is this sheet. A sheet unfortunately much abused, but observe. The lineaments identical. You can see how the longer-armed characters breathe through a type of sporule, exceptionally gauzy. And these commas, with their tails coughed off! Who could impersonate such a mannerism? A scrimshaw of the nervous system. These devious ropes of the nerves themselves. The ink is very close. The paper not identical, but very close. Of that period, no doubt of Warsaw manufacture, possibly Lvov . . ."

Adela did not stir. Heidi did not stir. These women were apathetic; lethargic. Probably it was what they had expected. They had known all along. They had believed all along. The verdict had only exhausted them; it was by now—so long awaited—a kind of soporific. Even Dr. Eklund did not appear to be aroused.

But there on the table lay the scattered *Messiah*. Retrieved. The original. *The Messiah*, spread out in its curiously rapturous Polish for anyone's bare blink. The original! Recovered; resurrected; redeemed. Lars, looking with all his strength, felt his own ordinary pupil consumed by a conflagration in the socket. As if copulating with an angel whose wings were on fire.

13

ALWAYS AFTERWARD—after the letters had collapsed
to char and flakes of ash—Lars regretted this animal urgency
that swept him through the scrambled pages of *The Messiah*.
Dr. Eklund was willing enough to concentrate on his pipe while
Lars tore through those layers of ruined papers. The two women
—Heidi dazed on her cot, Adela quiescent on the floor—
seemed suspended. They waited. You could not hear them
breathe. It was as if they had given up oxygen; or else had sup-
pressed the predilection for it.

Meanwhile Lars fell into the text with the force of a man
who throws himself against a glass wall. He crashed through it
to the other side, and what was there? Baroque arches and niches,
intricately hedged byways of a language so incised, so *bleeding*
—a touch could set off a hundred slicing blades—that it could
catch a traveler anywhere along the way with this knife or
that prong. Lars did not resist or hide; he let his flesh rip. Nothing
detained him, nothing slowed him down. The terrible speed of
his hunger, chewing through hook and blade, tongue and voice,
of the true *Messiah*! Rapacity, gluttony!

Always afterward Lars remembered the rising of his lamentation. It was as if he had been accumulating remorse even as he

fled through passage after passage. He could not contain what he met; he could not keep it. Amnesia descended with the opacity of a dropped hood. What he took he lost. And instantly grieved, because he could not keep it.

Adela was not there. The servant girl, sinister, elusive, brutal, who lurked in corridors and attics, in *Cinnamon Shops*, in *Sanatorium*—she was nowhere in *The Messiah*. This made Lars glad: a revenge against the self-important living Adela who leaned like a puppet against the leg of the table. *The Messiah* had annihilated her name.

Still, what Adela had told him was true: the order of the pages did not matter. These poor battered sheets were erratically paginated, some not numbered at all, and one eddying flowed into another; there were sequences and consequences, parallels and paradoxes, however you shuffled them. Lars thought of those mountain ranges growing out of the chasm of the world, along the bottommost spine of the sea, so platonically dark and deep that even the scuttling blindfish swim away, toward higher water—but within this overturned spittoon of an abyss are crisscrossing rivers, whirlpools twisting their foaming necks, multiple streams braiding upward, cascades sprouting rivulets like hairs, and a thousand shoots and sprays bombarding the oceanscape's peaks. So it was with the intelligence of *The Messiah*'s order and number and scheme of succession: everything voluminously overlapping, everything simultaneous and multiform.

But this understanding applied only to a consciousness of system. *The Messiah* was a waterless tract. No cloud, no mist, no fog; no well and no bucket; neither ocean nor droplet; no dribble or drizzle or trickle. No ichor, godly or ungodly, of any kind. It was desert-dry all through. It was equally bare of any dust of sky—no planet, no star, no galaxy, no heaven, no blue, no infinity—and this was odd, because *The Messiah*, insofar as it could be determined to be "about" anything (and Lars,

amnesiac, afterward forgot almost all of it), was about creation
and redemption. It was a work of cosmogony and entelechy. Like
everything else spilled out of the preternaturally cornucopian
eye of the genie whom Lars had only that morning dreamed of
as his own father, *The Messiah* had its "locality," its place, its
inch, its spot of tiny ground. The universe of *The Messiah* was
Drohobycz, a town in Galicia.

Adela was not in it. Yet it was not quite right to say Adela
was not in it. She was there, but not alive, and unnamed. At
first she appeared as a bald rag doll left on a shelf—the scalp,
however, was porcelain, and the lids could snap open and shut.
On another page this same flexible doll was transmuted into
rigidity: now she was a tailor's dummy, canvas over bent wires.
Elsewhere she had become one of those Mesopotamian priestly
statues carved out of stone only for the sake of their terrifying
smiles. Finally Lars took in that she had turned, with full purity
of intent, into an idol. Her eyes were conventional green jewels.
This idol, made of some artificial dead matter, was never called
Adela, and did not in any way hint at being Adela. Though
Lars could not claim that Adela was anywhere in the text, he
recognized her all the same.

Drohobycz was now wholly peopled (but this word was un-
suitable) by idols. Some were plump Buddhas in lotus position,
unable to walk or move. They were carried on litters by miniature
Egyptian figurines, several dozen for each litter. Others were
mammoth Easter Island heads. Another was the monolatrous
Ikhnaton, with his disease-deformed face and limbs, himself
elevated to an idol. A great many were in the shape of large stone
birds—falcons, eagles, vultures, hawks, oversized crows hewn
out of black marble. Each of these idols was considered to be a
great and powerful god or goddess, able to control the present and
future of Drohobycz, and especially the past. There was one
rather modest idol—it had the form of the owner of a drygoods
shop—who could alter the last hundred years of the history of

Drohobycz simply by the manipulation of a certain series of trouser buttons cleverly sewn into the flap of its caftan.

No human beings remained in Drohobycz; only hundreds and hundreds of idols. A few were contemptibly crude and ill-constructed, but most represented the inspired toil of armies of ingenious artisans, and there was actually a handful of master-works. The streets and shops were packed and milling with all these remarkable totems of wood, stone, pottery, silver and gold. Since there were no human beings to worship them, there was some confusion about their purpose. The more diffident among them, accordingly, undertook to adore the more aggressive; but at first this was not very typical. Each was accustomed to being regarded as sublime, each was expecting at any moment to discover a woman on her knees, a child bringing a basket of offerings, men in sacerdotal garments burning incense, or sacrificing a ram or even another human being; but there were no longer any human beings anywhere in Drohobycz. They had all gone on long, fatiguing journeys to other cities. All the former shop-keepers, for instance, were visiting their shopkeeper-cousins in Warsaw and Budapest. The high school teachers were touring the museums of Paris. Several would-be fiancées were languishing in London. The rest of the population was variously scattered, and could be rounded up, if need be, in Prague or Stockholm or Moscow or even as far away as New York, Montreal, and Tel Aviv.

The idols of Drohobycz were relatively passive and had no idea of how to go about rounding up their worshipers. It never occurred to any of them to do more than wander in and out of the town park, shuffle through the empty shops, and wait. It was as if every former inhabitant of Drohobycz had converted to atheism and fled. Religion had dried up in the churches as well as in the post office and the schools and the public library. And this was a pity, because the idols had never before been more beautifully polished, painted, and decorated than they were during their sojourn in Drohobycz. They were, to tell the truth, almost too enchanting, too seductive—which is probably why they started to bow to one another, and at length even to sacrifice to one another.

More and more frequently there were sacrificial bonfires all over Drohobycz. The taller and stronger idols began seizing the smaller and lesser idols and casting them into the flames. Bright-torsoed gods, and in particular the little Near Eastern goddesses with their fragile budding breasts and their necklaces fitted out with bits of mirror-burnished copper strung together on serpent-skin thongs, and occasionally even an exquisite miniature Venus-copy no bigger than a finger, were being chopped up or melted down to gratify the iron maw of some huge lazy Moloch. Day and night honeyed swirls of hot incense and the acrid smoky smell of roasting metal circled over Drohobycz.

The town was on fire, idols burning up idols in a frenzy of mutual adoration.

Then—matter-of-factly, with no fanfare—the Messiah arrived. (And almost immediately fell to pieces.)

His origin . . . no. You could not say "his" origin, or "her" origin, though the Messiah's description didn't quite justify an "it," either. Still, the neuter will have to suffice. The Messiah was alive, organic, palpitating with wild motion and disturbance —yet not like a robot, not like a machine. It was as if a fundamental internal member had set out to live on its own in the great world—a spleen, say, or a pancreas, or a bowel, or a brain. But this is only by way of hint and suggestiveness, not analogy or example. The Messiah's origin—or, at least, the roost it was reputed to have climbed out of—was the cellar of, of all places, the Drohobycz synagogue. A very old man had once lived down there for as long as anyone could remember. Generations knew that Moses the Righteous One, as he was called, slept on the mammoth bundle of hay that was both his merchandise and his shop. He was a vender of hay, and also a famous saint. Beggars came streaming to his cavern, and he sent them away with whatever he had in his pockets. Lately the cellar was, of course, vacant.

The idols believed that Moses the Righteous One's hay was somehow stuffed into the inmost composition of the Messiah, like a scarecrow. This was false. More than anything else, the Messiah (Lars noted) resembled a book—The Book, in fact, that in one of the tales in *Sanatorium pod Klepsydra* had been likened to *a huge cabbage rose: the petals, one by one, eyelid under eyelid, all blind, velvety, and dreamy.* This Book had also been set forth as *a postulate*; and again as *the authentic Book, the holy original, however degraded and humiliated at present.* In appearance it seemed to be fabricated of various commonplace inanimate materials, none of them costly or in any way precious —cotton, cardboard, glue, thread, and not a wisp of hay any-where. Its locomotion was dimly frightening, but also somewhat hobbled and limited: it had several hundred winglike sails that tossed themselves either clockwise or counterclockwise, like the arms of a windmill. But these numerous "arms" were, rather, more nearly flippers—altogether flat, freckled all over with inky markings, and reminiscent, surely, of turning pages. The flippers did indeed have the moist texture of petals, however, and their peculiar tattoos certainly put one in mind of some postulate recorded in an archaic signification—a type of cuneiform, per-haps, though it was impossible to say what this unreadable text might be proposing as thesis or axiom. When examined with extreme attention—better yet, when scrutinized through a magnifying glass (the author's assertion; there were no human eyes on the scene to do this)—the inky markings showed them-selves to be infinitely tiny and brilliantly worked drawings of these same idols that had taken hold of the town of Drohobycz. It was now clear that Drohobycz had been invaded by the char-acters of an unknown alphabet.

Meanwhile the structure itself, its stippled flippers continually revolving, sending out a grand ululation of wind, creaked with its own ancientness, about to break down, cave in, or simply fly apart—when, out of the caldron of that great wind, a small bird was suddenly flung up; it carried in its beak a single strand of dried hay.

It was a birth. The Messiah had given birth to a bird, and the moment the bird flew living out of the relentlessly wheeling contrivance that had been the Messiah, the thing—or organism —collapsed with the noise of vast crashings and crushings, cardboard like stone, cotton like bone, granite petal on brazen postulate: degraded and humiliated. The keen little bird, toiling, thrashed from idol to idol, exerting its fragile wing-muscles, and touching every idol with its bit of hay. And then there rose up out of Drohobycz the sound of lamentation and elegy, as the bonfires were extinguished, and the idols were dissolved into sparks by the tiny wand of hay flicked here and there by the poor thrashing bird, until the town was desolate, empty streets and empty shops and empty houses, and the flecks of sparks fading to ash.

The human beings—gone; the idols—gone; only this small beating bird born of an organism called the Messiah, and dim wails dying . . .

14

THERE WAS, Lars saw, a lie in the room.

"You didn't come for a translator," he told Adela. "It wasn't that. Even if I could."

"Even if you could." Dr. Eklund busied himself gathering up the pages of *The Messiah*. He reached his bulky sea captain's arm down to the floor after the brass amphora; his sleeve, swinging on its own, gave Adela's ear a quick slap. "You see? There you have it, miss. In my judgment there's no doubt, and I say it again—none. The hand of the artist."

"The hand," Heidi echoed, "of the artist." It seemed to Lars he was in the kitchen of Sleeping Beauty's castle, when the trance is broken and all the pots begin to boil again. It was as if Heidi had switched herself back on. And what was it, after all, that had put these women into trance?

Adela—bounced out of somnolence—had snatched the sheets from Dr. Eklund and was stuffing them, in bunches, back into the brass amphora.

"No, my dear, this is not the way. You are mishandling matter valuable in the extreme—"

"Immensely valuable. Immensely, immensely," Heidi said.

"Don't tell me that. I'm the one who found them! I'm the

one they belong to. I'm the daughter of the man who *wrote* them."

Heidi threw out her doglike laugh.

"This man's papers belong to the world," Dr. Eklund said.

"*He* said"—Adela shot her arrow at Lars—"they belong to *him*."

"Please. No rancor. The question is what is to be done. A decision, yes? We must come to a decision."

So Dr. Eklund too had a "we."

"I'm out of it," Lars said.

"Oh, you're *in* it. Lars, you're definitely in it," Heidi argued. "Look how you're involved!"

"If he kept my key," Dr. Eklund said.

"If he kept my hat," Adela said.

How alike their two voices were!

Lars scoffed: "*She* said she was looking for a translator."

"Translation is the least of it," Heidi said. "Stockholm's swarming with Polish translators."

"The Princess."

"Better than that."

"Dr. Eklund, then."

"I told you, he has more important things."

Match after failed match; Dr. Eklund was tending his pipe again. "This work," he announced, "will live to enter every language on the planet."

"The planet?" Heidi said. "Put the planet aside, Olle, and think of Stockholm."

"Yes, start with Stockholm," Adela said.

Dr. Eklund intervened: "My dear Adela—Adela? Is it Adela?"

"Adela," Heidi said.

"Undoubtedly you bring us this manuscript with a history attached. A story, yes? This fellow doesn't believe it, I see that. Undoubtedly there is a story, and why shouldn't we believe it?

No manuscript sans story, yes? And this one in particular. If you told me the story I promise you I would believe it. But whatever the story, whatever the history, whatever your attachment or devotion—"

"She says she's the daughter," Heidi remarked: detached.

"—now is the time to relinquish it."

"Look at Lars! *He's* relinquished everything," Heidi said.

"For the sake of the world," Dr. Eklund said—an actor's flourish.

"For the sake of the world!" Adela said. "He'll say anything. He's admitted he's a liar. He had to, he didn't have a leg to stand on. And when I told him how I got the manuscript—well, he collapsed, that's all. He had to."

All this was true; Lars was silent.

"Poor Lars," Heidi said. She did not defend him now. "But now that you've had a look at it?" And waited.

She waited; Lars understood why. She meant him—in the wake of his great wish—to tell what he thought. He had got his great wish. He had stormed the precincts of *The Messiah.* Heidi more than anyone—no; Heidi alone, only Heidi!—knew the secret furnace of his will; she had called it his concentration, his mania. She was the old partner of his desire; of his intuition. She alone could fathom how it must be for him to flood his eyes with that text—that very text—the thing itself, the words, the syllables, the letters! The letters left their drifting afterimages on his retinas. But he could not take in those figurines—it was as if the Polish had escaped him. Lost. What was in *The Messiah?* Lost! Chips of dream.

It was nearly as if he had stumbled into someone else's dream. Whose? Was it Adela's? Heidi's? These women in trance: he had dreamed their dream. He could not remember what he had read five minutes ago. A perplexity. Amulets, a contraption, a bird . . . fragments of some vagrant insub-stantiality, folklorish remnants; a passage of oxygen-deprivation perhaps. It had receded, whatever it was—he retained nothing, nothing lingered: only the faintest tremor of some strenuous force. Mute imprint of noise—a city falling, crumbling, his own moans, relentless lamentation. Sound of shooting. Amnesia. Lost. Nothing remained.

Lamentation remained. Elegy after great pain. That despoiling, withdrawing light, a lightning-explosion. As though—for an inch of time—he had penetrated into the entrails, the inmost anatomy, of that eye. Whoever had dipped into the ink that covered the pages of *The Messiah* had dipped into the vitreous gelatin of that sufficing eye.

Dr. Eklund held up a hand. His rings blazed their sea-chest glints. "What is necessary, what we must decide before anything else, is the heralding, you see? The annunciation."

"People have to be made to believe it. No one's going to believe it, that's the thing," Heidi said.

Dr. Eklund shone: his fingers, his buttons, his bald crown, his big glowing face with its bright lenses. "The good news must be given out. That *The Messiah* is here. Uncovered. Found. That it exists."

"People have to be *told* it exists," Heidi pressed. "If it's not believed in, it might as well not exist."

"That sounds like God," Lars said. He was bewildered. There was a lie in the room—some entanglement, a cat's cradle gone wild, and Dr. Eklund's coruscating rings and spectacles enmeshed in the strings. Lars could not tell whether the knots were worsening or unraveling. Across from him Adela stood, the brass amphora in her arms; *The Messiah* was in it. It made him think of a mummy in a case, or else a round baby.

He watched her circle the little back-room space with her burden. Dr. Eklund had tried to make her give it up. Heidi had tried. She would not so much as set it down.

"Let the world have it!" she said. "Oh yes! Well, how is the world going to know? Who's going to believe it?"

It troubled Lars that Adela said only what the others said. Even while resisting them, she used Heidi's words; she used Dr. Eklund's.

"*You* believe it. You to begin with," Heidi told her. "After all, don't we begin with you? You came to find out for yourself. You came to *consult*. Anyone can palm off anything on anybody if they've got a good enough story."

"My dear woman, this masterwork? This beautiful text of genius, this holy art? It could no more pass for spurious than"— Dr. Eklund sent his reconnoitering look straight over to Lars— "than the true Creator of the Universe could pass for a philosopher's idea."

"All the same," Heidi said, "people have to be made to believe in it."

Lars hesitated; he considered. "I told them at the *Morgontörn*," he said finally. "I mentioned it over there."

"Aha! Bravo!" Dr. Eklund cried.

Adela said sourly, "You were premature."

Heidi asked: "You told them at your paper? About *The Messiah*?"

"I told them it was found."

"But you didn't know—"

"I told them anyway. I told Nilsson—he runs the book section."

"And what did he say?"

"He didn't believe me. No one did. I didn't believe it then myself. It was a sort of daydream."

"You see how he'll say anything to anyone," Adela said.

"But now! Lars! You've had your look. You've seen it with your own eyes. The original, *nicht wahr*? Here it is, safe in a jar. In a jar, God help us. Like one of those Dead Sea things—"

"Those were clay. I have to protect what's mine," Adela said.

"All your life you've waited for it. You've persisted." Heidi extended her sheeplike head. He saw how old and earnest she was—decaying, pleading, wounded. That fence. The shooting. She wanted him to tell what he thought. "*The Messiah* exists, you've taken it in. Now it's in your power."

"My power? I have no power." How pointless she was: *The Messiah* was in Adela's power; or, at least, in her grip. As for him, he had taken in *some*thing, yes—something too quickly, something too hotly—like a man half-blinded, who can descry only the flat light, not the characters on a page. Or he had swallowed it down like a priest, the priest of some passionate sect, for whom scripture is subordinate to the hour of sacral access. Awe consumes any brand that ignites it: was it the true *Messiah* he had taken in, or only the Walpurgisnacht caravan of his private menagerie trekking across his poor fevered brain-pan?

"He's in your hands. The author of *The Messiah*."

"I told you, I've quit. I'm finished. He's not mine. I can't hold on to him. My hands," he said, turning them over to show her his white palms, "are empty."

"No, no, think! Think how you've got the means."

"You've got that column," Adela said abruptly. "You write those reviews. You've got Mondays."

"You can let them know," Dr. Eklund said. "You can deliver up some stupendous thing. You can explain."

"You can be *use*ful," Heidi said. "If you're shrewd about it. If you want to restore to the world what belongs to the world. If you believe in it yourself."

The world, the world—they all three spoke of the world. What speechifiers! They were mad for the world. They had something in mind for the world. The world had put them in perfect agreement. Lars in his newest bewilderment felt how he was marveling at it: the sulphurous tail of some underlying unanimity. To what did it attach itself?

Dr. Eklund's matches—the same smothered crash of spark after spark, every match in concert with every other, all designed to light a recalcitrant fire in the great man's pipe.

Toll of a gong, small and sharp. Adela clattering the brass amphora down at last.

"You can take the manuscript if you like," she offered—it was Dr. Eklund's rawest stage voice—"even before it's translated. To show it. That it exists. Translation's the least of it—you can show it at your paper if you want."

How he wanted to knock her down!

"She'll let you take it now, you know," said Dr. Eklund, approving.

"There's no question she'll let you take it. You're the one to do it." Heidi's web was loosening more and more—she was sliding from placating to out-and-out importuning. "It's just what Dr. Eklund said—you're the only one in Stockholm who *can*. You've got the reputation for it. It's what people expect—you're an introducer, you pave the way. An usher—you're the only one who dares or cares. You've brought in all those difficult creatures—all those Central Europeans we've always got on order! Those Czechs and Poles! Yugoslavians and Hungarians! You've made everyone notice. Mr. Hemlig and Mr. Fiskyngel, for instance—they rely on you to alert them. You wake them up. You shake them up. You make them *see*."

It was a speech, a declamation—her mouth was tumultuous: her old woman's disorderly gold teeth. She was imploring him. There was something he was intended for. A quaver had entered her nostrils.

Dr. Eklund, meanwhile, was nodding his big face up and down, cheering her on like a human baton. "Difficult creatures!" he said admiringly. "You were born to it, Mr. Andemening. Granted it's elusive—what work of art isn't? But you've absorbed it. We've allowed you to absorb it. You've had our silence. What we need from you now is some word. A judgment.

Is it worthy? Is it beautiful? Will you embrace it? We need to have your sounding."

"We need to have your column," Adela said. Did Adela too have her "we"? They all three had a "we"—the same one. They adhered. They were a cabal; a family. His column! His unread and sequestered Mondays—she was ridiculing him. Yet he understood she was not. It came to him—incompletely, slowly, stupidly—that they were, the three of them, in some logical alliance: they had a common principle. Clearly they intended him for something. He was a pipe they were all three attempting to kindle. What was smoldering in this place was not so much a lie as a latency. It was their private idea. What they wanted from him was his own day of the week. Monday was the whole purpose of his standing just where he was standing. He was standing a foot from Heidi's little back-room table—on which Adela, with the ringing of some weighty doubloon, had half a minute ago settled *The Messiah* in its brass vessel. For the sake of Monday he had been given Dr. Eklund's key. For the sake of Monday Adela had invaded his flat. For the sake of Monday he had been made to come and go, and then to stay.

He saw everything exactly. They had done everything to lure him into believing *The Messiah* was false, in order to persuade him it was genuine. They had sent him Adela with her story, to mock the fraudulent son with the fraudulent daughter. An artificial sister! Family mockery. He had fallen among players; among plotters.

"Dr. Eklund," he charged—he was breathing like a runner—"why do you say you're Dr. Eklund?"

"He isn't anyone else," Heidi said. "Who else should he be?"

"Someone who fits the name."

"We poor wanderers with our pitiful accents, yes?" Dr. Eklund said.

"It's fakery."

"In Rome do as the Romans." Dr. Eklund pulled vainly on

his pipe, meditating. "In this country they are so shy with foreigners. It goes much better not to contradict the feelings of a shy people."

"Refugee impostor," Lars shot out.

"Lars, Lars," Heidi begged.

Dr. Eklund placidly lit another match. "A name is such a little thing. A ribbon. A modest pennant. A harmless decoration. I myself was born Eckstein."

The ape in Lars's chest sprang awake with an electric shudder and hurled itself across his ribs. Harmless! How hard it was to breathe, to breathe in and out! There was, however, illumination. He saw everything exactly. He said the chosen syllables to himself: *Lazarus Baruch. Lars Andemening.*

"I made up my name. I made up my father."

His father out of libraries, his name out of dictionaries.

"Dr. Eklund knows all this. You can't mind that I told him your theory of paternity? You're the one who told Adela."

Adela surrendered to what seemed to be her duty: "It doesn't matter to him, he'll say anything." But she had grown as dull as an obedient child.

"The immersion. The concentration. What it took to put on those robes—the ascent! Admirable," Dr. Eklund trumpeted. "For an ordinary Alter Eckstein to jump into Stockholm and start calling himself Olle Eklund—nothing. Purely nothing. There's no nerve to it. I've never had a nervous hour over it. But you! Gilgul! Karma! Transmigration of an impassioned soul! Mr. Andemening," he finished, "I'll tell you what it makes you. Do you understand what it makes you? It makes you just our man."

Heidi put in, "Because of Monday."

"Two or three of those columns, that's the way. Holy space. Fill it with the news. You've done exalted things there. The cognoscenti know what you've done, don't think they're not aware. You've got your little following—you're just the one to make it happen."

"I'm just the one to bring on *The Messiah*." The sound of it was as flat as if someone had asked him the time.

"Isn't that what you've lived for?" Heidi said.

"Fakery. I've lived for fakery."

"But you've stopped. You've quit."

"*You* haven't. You said yourself you're not quitting, Mrs. Eklund."

"It's a question of recognition. We've got the original, right here—you saw it. A long look, you can't complain. What you can *do* for it! No one knows better than you. You had your hands on it."

His transient little fear. His hands were hot. His fingers were heating up like the staves of a fence on fire.

"*The Messiah* went into the camps with its keeper." Lars shook: the ape had him by the throat. "That's all that could have happened, nothing else. *The Messiah* was burned up in those places. Behind those fences, in those ovens. It was burned, Mrs. Eklund, burned!"

"You don't believe your own two eyes? You had it in your own two hands! You don't believe Dr. Eklund? Dr. Eklund's dealt with these situations all over, he's done this sort of work in dozens of countries—"

"*Dealt* with them. I'll bet he's dealt with them. Where there's fire there's a match. Those hospital rounds. The Danish prima ballerina. A wheeler-dealer in shady manuscripts, that's what it's about."

"You're a baby, Lars. You don't understand any of it."

"Shady, well, well," Dr. Eklund said. "It's what you would call a little awning. Mrs. Eklund knows I don't like it when she gives things away, so she rolls down this little awning."

Dr. Eklund got up out of his chair and began to wander—

he picked up the kettle from the stove, swung it to hear how much water was left in it, and put it back again. In this snug and narrow galley he was massively seaworthy—more like a ship than its captain. The daffodil lamp on its stalk might have been another pipe he was about to poke between his teeth. He had anyhow lost interest in his pipe; he was distracted; he had let it go out.

"Anything original—anything that's a masterwork, you know —needs a little awning to begin with. If you want to talk about shady, I don't deny there are transactions that can't be negotiated in the noonday sun. Too much light rots the merchandise. On the other hand, after three or four decades in the shade a text becomes diffident. Bashful, you might say. Sometimes it takes persuasion to lure it out of hiding. It could be in francs or marks or rubles or kroner, whatever's suitable. The texts don't care. The money brightens them and they want to show how brave they are. Then their heads slide out. If only I had such money of my own."

"There you are. You've heard it all," Heidi said. "Now you can stop being a baby about these things. As if those Warsaw items got here out of the blue! If not for Dr. Eklund's *network*—"

"No, no," Dr. Eklund broke in. "In the beginning the blue is all there is. Everything comes out of the blue. Here's *The Messiah*, out of the blue." He clinked his rings against the brass amphora: what pealed out was the trill of an heirloom chime— the striking of some old family clock. "And this fine woman— this nervous noble handsome woman—now isn't *she* out of the blue?"

He had taken Adela by the shoulders; it was ludicrous how he hunched down his own shoulders to put his long face in the way of hers. There was something curiously practiced in the exchange of light that passed between their pairs of eyes. The two foreheads closed brow to brow: the channel midway might have been harboring signals. Or else nothing more than the blinking crescents of Dr. Eklund's lenses, throwing off reflections. His captain's stare of ownership, his potent pirate's touch—he had already released one half of her, and was stroking the side of her nose. No, inconceivable: he was lifting away a single hair that was intruding there. A peculiarly private act, like a cat that licks its own paw clean—there was a strain of habituation in it. Adela hardly minded; she barely noticed. She was intent on her mood: she was inured to this large-fingered mechanical caress; it appeared to toughen the resistant line of her lip. It was only her lip that was resisting; she was turning more and more docile. She resembled someone who has done her duty. They had been in combination before, Adela and Dr. Eklund—was such a thing possible? They had the accommodation of an old couple; it didn't count that Dr. Eklund was surely three decades in advance in the sea of life. Something had been compounded between them: something more abrasive than mere familiarity. Had they once been lovers, had this been her duty, now far behind her? The man still liked the woman; the woman didn't like the man. But she lent herself. She obeyed.

Her head pulled back; she was squirming herself loose. A resentful childish movement. A woman of forty, and she wriggled like a child. It put Lars in mind of Karin's small slippery body, sad years ago, ripping free of him; it had been Ulrika's game to provoke Karin against him. Adela was pliant enough; it was only her lip that was hard. Her head, pulling back, was all at once new: he took in the graven trenches at the roots of her eyes, the white thistles speckled through her hair, the momentary glimmer of child—it was all new. She was not what she had been. He had imagined himself a looking-glass Adela; he had imagined her his sister. She was not his sister. A conspiratorial illusion. She was as unlike him as it was in the power of nature to contrive. She belonged to another line. His mother—that omission—was not her mother, whoever her mother might be. Whoever had fathered him had not fathered her.

Then he saw—a wind flew through his brain—who had fathered her.

Adela was released. Dr. Eklund had released her. She stood a little to the side of him. She was not willing to meet his look again.

Heidi let herself down on her cot and sighed. "Can't we come to an agreement? All you have to do is agree."

"I don't know what you want me to agree to," Lars said.

"You do know. You know exactly."

"There's money in it," Adela said thinly; but this mildness and thinness held a fleeting brutality, like faint lightning far away.

"The value of the sublime," Dr. Eklund said.

Their plausibly concocting voices—they might have been two urns of the same ancestry, shape for shape, turn for turn.

"It wouldn't be out of your own brain," Heidi said. "It wouldn't be like that eye—it's something you could set straight out in the light. As solid as that jar."

"Again this eye. What is this eye?" Dr. Eklund asked.

"Don't talk about it," Lars said roughly. "Didn't I tell you it's over and done with?"

Adela hung back; she was very quiet. Lars noticed for the first time how her nose showed a narrow sharp bone. Dr. Eklund's was different. The puny centerpiece of Dr. Eklund's great spread-out face was a quick round spurt of tallow sliced through by two long slashes. So it wasn't to be found *there*: the rest of the likeness. Then it might be somewhere else, it might be something altogether other—some way of starting or stopping this or that muscle. It wasn't in their features—not nose or lip or eye. Lars didn't know where it was. It was enough that he felt it, and not only in their voices. Of their voices he was certain.

"It's true," he said.

"Keep away," Adela said.

But he had begun. He was driving toward her. It wasn't the

ape. The ape was dead; its carcass was a dead weight on his lung. It was himself now, it was the blast of his own force that drove him.

"Oh yes, it's true, I can see for myself it's true, and I apologize."

"There!" said Heidi. "I told you he'd apologize!"

"I didn't think it was true, but now I see it is. It's just the way you said it was. You're the daughter."

"Don't come *near* me," Adela said.

He raised his arm. He knew how terrible his arm was, high up—how he wanted to knock her down! How he wanted to stamp on her face, on the beautiful little bird-bone of her nose! How he wanted to trample on the dove-colored feathers of her hair!

"You're the daughter of the author of *The Messiah*, that's who you are. And the author of *The Messiah* is Dr. Eklund." An ugly noise went rattling against the brass amphora like a thrown coin: his old croak, or knot, or rasp, or whatever it was: the ape's sprawling carcass cast loose. "It's a forgery, isn't it? Mrs. Eklund, it's a forgery, admit it! It's a forgery, and you want me to pass it off for you. To legitimate it. How easy it is, I'm just the one to do it! To pass it into the world, admit it!"

"What a spiteful version you've got," Heidi sent out from her cot; but she was appealing to Dr. Eklund.

Lars turned on Adela: "*Your* version's not the one."

"What do you know about Drohobycz? What's Drohobycz to you?" Adela said in her new thin voice, with its distant dim flashes. His arm was high up. She was under his lifted arm. The daffodil spilled out its yellow syrup, and his arm shadowed her mouth and neck and chin; and hadn't her own arms made a darkness over his quilt, hadn't she blotted out his father's eye with her outstretched arms?

"Let the barbarian dare," Dr. Eklund warned, "and the barbarian pays."

"I'm the barbarian? I'm the one who pays?" Lars yelled.

"In the long run, if you're willing"—but Heidi's crooked golden mouth was plunged into her pillow—"it's going to pay."

"I'll show you what pays, I'll show you"—and beat his arm through a descending gale, the fingers hooked, the fingers on fire, ready to pluck, sweeping past the blackening scorn of Adela's lightning eyes—how he wanted to pluck them out, to dig them out with his fingernails, to pound on her rustling dove-like head, how he wanted to break her, to plunder her face, how she had toyed with him, how she had blotted out his father's eye, how she had orphaned him, how she had mocked and nullified the author of *The Messiah.* . . . It was a tiny stick he dived for instead: one of Dr. Eklund's matches on the little back-room table, dropped near the base of the brass amphora.

The first one was no good. The tip was charred; it was burnt out. The table was littered with these tiny charred sticks. He found a clean unused one and struck it and threw it down the throat of the brass amphora and watched the steeple of fire rise straight out of it like the flame from an ogre's nostril. The jar shook, it roared, it seemed to howl; it was as if an unholy beast were rocking in there, drubbing on the inside walls, howling out its dying.

Adela was on the floor—flogged, crumpled, thrashed. He had not touched her even with the brush of his little finger. But her head was twisted round: the vertical trenches took on the bitter horizontal look of an equal sign. Her bird-bone nose streamed. "There's your priest, you called him priest—"

"Douse it, douse it!" Dr. Eklund commanded.

But Heidi had already catapulted from her cot to the kettle on the stove, and was pouring water into the flaming neck of the brass amphora. The fire fought back and would not give way; the steeple spurted higher, the roaring gargled louder, the jar went on chattering and boiling, battering the little table, dancing across it like a demon. It danced to the edge of the table and crashed down an inch from the heap that was Adela.

"My shop! The whole place may catch, my God!"

"Move! Watch your hair! Out of the way!" With all the orderly brutishness of his captain's shoe Dr. Eklund kicked at Adela to make her roll.

She rolled and moaned.

"Quiet, keep quiet, can't you? Olle, fill it again, fill it," and handed over the kettle to Dr. Eklund; meanwhile Heidi stamped on the big burned cabbage leaves that were creeping out of the brass amphora—curling black sheets with delicately crimped ruffs glowing red. A flood came shooing down through the smoke. "There, we've got it, fill it again—"

The brass amphora had turned black at the lip: it wobbled, sputtered, expired; it smoked and smoked. The rivers flying down its hot flanks steamed among cinders. The smoke rummaged.

Heidi flailed at her eyes with a piece of her sleeve. "You've put us inside a chimney! Spiteful! Deranged!"

Dr. Eklund said coldly: "Arson."

"You've sizzled us!"

Adela murmured from the floor, "Didn't I say he'd do anything—"

"Fake," Lars said.

"And aren't you the one who forged his father? Refugee impostor! The pot," Heidi blazed at him, "calling the kettle black."

"Barbarian." Dr. Eklund spat down on the blackened amphora: a sneeze of steam leaped up. "*I* could make that? I, I? A seraph made it! Idiocy—*I* could make that? Instinct's the maker! Transfiguration, is this your belief? Conspiracy gives birth to a masterwork? You had your look, you saw! You think what's born sublime can be connived at? How? How, without that dead man's genius? What is there to empower such an impersonation?" The smoke snatched him then; the sea captain was now a Chinese mandarin in the grip of an encrusted language moving through powerful forms; he fell into a long clamor of coughing. He coughed and whitened. "Do you think there is a magical eye that drops from heaven to inspire? Barbarian, where is such an eye?"

"Mrs. Eklund," Lars addressed her, "it isn't just the shop, is it? There's more to the family business than just the shop." His feet churned through puddles, he felt himself drenched in smoke. "It isn't only getting people in and getting people out—it's not even a matter of *taking* people in, that's the wonder. You took *me* in—you hooked me practically from the start. A pack of swindlers, I don't care—that's not the family business. You want to be in competition with God, that's the thing."

Adela lifted her wild face. A bloody rip across the blade of the frail nose. It wasn't Lars's work; not even the lick of his burning little finger. It was her father who had smashed her. The ferocious kick of the author of *The Messiah*.

Dr. Eklund's head shone like a polished shield. He tore his glasses from his ears; and there it was, without warning—the likeness. It wasn't in any particular inch of him. It was all over —the resemblance, the pulse of ancestry. His naked eyes spilled catastrophe: he had nothing to defend him now, not his rings, not the militant glitter of his sailor's buttons. His big scraped face with its awful nostril-craters rambled on, a worn old landscape lost to any habitation. Wild, wild. Adela's look exactly, at last.

15

AT FIVE O'CLOCK in the afternoon a little more than seven months after the fire in the brass amphora—the stewpot was just disbanding—a woman named Elsa Vaz, accompanied by a little boy, came to see Lars Andemening at the *Morgontörn*. He had his own cubicle now. It was a small bare box, with sides made of beaverboard, fitted out with a splintered table (formerly Nilsson's), a pink china mug (indistinguishable from Anders's), a typewriter, a coffeepot, and a chair covered with a torn and lumpy cushion. Plaster dust thickened the air—all the walls on the top floor of the *Morgontörn* were being broken open for new wiring. Nilsson had announced the installation of a whole row of computer terminals: the staff of the *Morgontörn* couldn't expect to catch up with *Expressen*, of course, but at least they could say hello to the century they were living in—in deference to which Nilsson had acquired a resplendent new desk fabricated entirely out of a substance hitherto used exclusively on the underside of the noses of space capsules.

Elsa Vaz explained to Lars that she had first gone to his old flat, only to learn that he had moved out some time ago. He pinched his fitful eyeglasses back into position (they took getting used to) and retorted that she might have telephoned him: he had a large apartment on Bergsundsstrand, not far from where Nellie Sachs had once resided; a civilized street, and didn't civilized people telephone before barging right on into someone's office? That fool of a girl downstairs! To have allowed Elsa Vaz to burst in on him, and with a child! After all, he kept rigid enough hours, had plenty of reading to push through, and couldn't sustain any kind of interruption: he had his Monday space to attend to, not to mention the masses of mail it brought him.

The little boy—he seemed to be about six years old—was struggling with a cold, miserably scrubbing away at himself with one or the other of two big white handkerchiefs, and clutching at the woman's knees. He went on shivering and occasionally sneezing, huddling into his own shoulders. They poked up: a pair of small sharp peaks surrounding a nutlike head.

Lars drew back, thinking of the germs. "Isn't he too sick to be out?"

"There's no one to leave him with—we're in a sort of rooming house." The familiar recalcitrance. It reminded him of his old distrust. "And anyhow the poor thing would feel lost. He speaks only Portuguese."

"Why not park him in the shop? They can manage anything over there."

"She's left Stockholm, didn't you know?"

He sent out an impartial stare. "How would I?"

"The shop is sold."

"I never pass that way." He concentrated on her face; it was not as he remembered it. "I never thought she'd give it up."

"He made her. He said it was enough. They've gone to live in Antwerp. The opportunities are better there."

The boy gave out a quick animal sob, followed by an incomprehensible demand in a language that—whatever it was—wasn't Portuguese. French? Polish? The woman said, "Will you let me sit down? Then I can take him on my lap."

Lars unwillingly surrendered his chair. "The opportunities," he echoed, and stood watching her arrange her skirt into a nest for the child. "You understand what it is, I've got my deadline breathing down my neck—"

"I've been reading you since I came. You've gotten just like the others," she announced.

"I'm told I've taken on a touch of fame."

"You're an ordinary reviewer."

"Even a reviewer can have a reputation."

"Last Monday a detective novel. The Monday before—I don't remember, was it the autobiography of some film star?"

"Then you've been in town two weeks," he said.

She laughed straight over the child's head. "There's an advantage to detective novels! But no, we've been here nearly three. The first week we didn't arrive till Wednesday."

"On business," he concluded. "Opportunities. You're his courier."

"Say whatever you please."

"You've got a different name now."

"I have all different names, it stands to reason."

"For different jobs?" He looked down at the boy; he had shut his eyes, but the lids were fat and red. "Is there a part for him?"

A pounding, just then, on one of the beaverboard partitions: it was Gunnar Hemlig, dropping off the mail. "Nilsson said to give you this"—he threw down a box overflowing with envelopes and whisked himself off. He had no word for Lars. Anders when encountered was almost as silent.

Lars had affronted them; they burned against him. He had put back all those things he had once pushed aside. It wasn't only the question of the furniture he was stuffing his new flat with—the stewpot had gone through this long before. He had a telephone attached to an automatic answering machine; he had a typewriter in his cubicle, like the rest of them, but at home he had a word processor with a screen that showered down green letters from Japan, and an electronic printer that typed with phantom fingers at a speed equal to the fall of the sun at the world's end. Nilsson was automating the *Morgontörn*, but Lars Andemening was robotizing himself. He kept—this was the stewpot's view of it—a robot woman under his bed. She was stored in an old vodka case. In the middle of the night Lars smacked a button and she clicked herself into position, constructing herself part by part. She was made mainly of styrofoam and hinged with old wedding rings bought wholesale from a divorce lawyer who had batches of them; the only task she required of Lars was to rouge her pale porous cheeks and to satisfy her vibrations.

Thus the stewpot, simmering. Nilsson was contemplating an extra day's spot for Lars, they said, to add on to his Mondays. He was fast; he was fluent; he had begun to keep regular hours and seldom prowled in the office after midnight. He was reformed, recovered; he had recovered from his old ailment. He was taking the reviewing business seriously. He had, it appeared, given up existential dread; he had given up those indecipherables that steam up from the stomach-hole of Central Europe; he was sticking to the Swedes and the more companionable Americans; you never heard him pronounce Kiš or Canetti or Musil or Broch; his tongue was free of Kafka. He was finished with all those grotesqueries. He was like a man in a coma who has unexpectedly come to, having been declared asleep for life, and who has resumed his normal rounds. The very routine of it seems extraordinary.

The stewpot boiled, but placidly; it had attenuated; by now it showed the mildest minor froth. In the last half year, though it had never taken the smallest notice of him before, Lars had grown to be the stewpot's steadiest habit. It was, in fact, Gunnar Hemlig and Anders Fiskyngel who had initiated this newest seething—it fell to them, no one knew why, Lars least of all.

Gunnar and Anders were suddenly Lars Andemening's cele-
brants in the rite of the stewpot—the stewpot in its frenzied
prime. Gunnar in particular relished the grand comedy of it—
how Lars, that beautiful soul, with his skinny nose up to the hilt
in belles-lettres, had been hoodwinked by a family of swindlers,
forgers, thieves, lovers of high art, symbolists! Entrapped and
consumed—their demonic fragrances, their sweet lures and ruses!
But no, the point was, Anders argued back, that these beauties
were nothing homegrown: a pack of Poles, a gang of outlanders,
six or eight of them, four Turks, two Portuguese, possibly some
gypsies. Sven Strömberg's lover tugged at her mannish collar
and picked up the thread: gypsies, yes, definitely a gypsy girl
among them, on the brown skin of whose silken back had been
tattooed—in infancy, in tiny green letters—a missing Psalm,
omitted by the generation of the Canonizers, that had been
traveling for centuries from back to back of certain young
women in certain Romany tribes, young women with split
tongues, born mute. As these dusky chosen infants grew, the
grass-bright letters expanded over their torsos; through insidious
means and for a magnanimous fee (hence the big new flat, the
new furniture, the robot appliances), Lars had been approached
to transcribe: he was seized, willy-nilly, being peculiarly eligible,
according to the ancient forms, since the girl who currently carried the Psalm engraved even in the delta of her buttocks was his
own stolen daughter. . . . Sven Strömberg's version was simpler.
The chief of the swindlers was Olof Flodcrantz in disguise.

Thus the stewpot, laughing. Gunnar and Anders observed
that these clownings were only a little bit at the expense of poor
dim duped Lars. Lars bruised and overthrown. So much for
exaltation, so much for the private ecstasies of the visionary!—he
had had his lesson. He was humbled and would henceforth
consent to walk among men again.

Yet abruptly the stewpot turned from boiling Lars to throwing its arms around his shoulders. The cackle of satire softened.

They chaffed him instead; he was a comrade. Gunnar and Anders, unprepared for this alteration of spirit, watched Lars, with his graying head and baby cheeks, rising. They looked again: somehow he wasn't so much fixed in earliness as he used to be; you could tell at a glance he wasn't a boy. Impossible to mistake him now for anything but a man of middling years—those grooves dug out in the space between the eyebrows, those beginning wadis that ran from the ends of the mouth downward toward the faint bulge at either side of the jaw . . . he was putting on weight. He couldn't negotiate a paragraph without his reading glasses. And still he was rising. It was as if a wraith of smoke, too elusive for the keenest camera, had all at once solidified into a statue: Lars was *there*. Monday's customers were waking up; they wrote him letters. They wrote him six or seven letters; then they wrote him dozens. He overtook Gunnar, he overtook Anders; he had more letters than anyone. He wasn't comical, he wasn't contentious—what could you say he *was*? Whatever he was, he produced an excess of it: Nilsson was ready to let him spill over the brink into Tuesday. It doubled his pay, and he took it as innocently as if he deserved it. They considered his prose: was there a trick in it; was it something no one could catch him at?

One night Gunnar thought he saw it. Lars had stopped purifying his life. This absence, this cessation, had the effect of an ingredient. The ingredient was the opposite of purification. It gratified intensely, it flowed out over almost everyone; it was the rosiest of mirrors; it flattered.

"And what is this fabled ingredient?" Anders inquired, returning from the tap. He no longer asked Lars to fetch him water: Lars had risen; and besides, nowadays you couldn't count on finding Lars when the mice were out. He was doing something else with his nights. As for the mice, Nilsson was arranging for the exterminators to come as soon as the electricians were done. The broken walls had exposed their nests.

"Mediocrity," Gunnar said.

They were not spiteful men, but they recognized the importance of cutting Lars dead. What else do you do with a fellow who prospers on scandal? Olof Flodcrantz had crept back from Finland, but at least he had vanished south to a job in Malmö; he made himself scarce. He didn't insult people by slamming himself like a beam in their eyes.

They waited for the stewpot to turn. The stewpot always turns. It swallows up. It casts out. It boils on.

16

T H E *Morgontörn* W A S emptying out. The electricians and their sledgehammers were long gone. They had begun at eight o'clock that morning by thundering open craters in the walls; until half an hour before lunch the ancient upper storeys of the *Morgontörn* were convulsed. Then the electricians had dematerialized. The secretaries were just now on their way out, fluttering down the stairs like confetti. Nilsson was rocketing shut the fine new drawers of his astral desk. The elevator, like the clapper of a bell striking the sides of the shaft, was heard to ring him perilously down to the street. Not a relic of the stewpot remained: not even the lees. Gunnar was already across the square, having his monthly tea with the Librarian of the Academy, an event calculated to impress the stewpot, if only it would allow him the chance to tell—what a bitterness, that it currently had ears only for the life and works of Lars Andemening! Anders had taken the bus home to the fossildom of his prehistoric household: the primordial stepfather, the antediluvian aunt.

The child, meanwhile, had fallen asleep with his mouth narrowly tubed—enough to let out a periodic snore, incongruous with such a small frame. The snore was leonine.

Her face was not as he remembered it. In half a year she had—he would not say toughened; but there was a brazen look now. He didn't mean that old grain of stubbornness, he didn't mean impudence; what he had in mind was the opposite. She seemed desperately still: *formed*: a figure cast out of some elemental metal. A motionless pietà, clear as copper—it might have been the influence of the boy in her lap. As for the boy's snore—it was as if she held a live trumpet that might go off at any moment.

"Why this rooming house?" he challenged her. "I thought you'd have plenty of money, you people. Why not a nice posh place within walking distance of the Café Opera? What cakes! You've done the little fellow an injustice."

She set her lips against the boy's forehead. "He's getting a fever."

"Unless the rooming house is part of the scenery? An apt effect?"

"You think anything I do is playacting."

"Anything I know of. They've roped you in. You do what's expected."

"He was all right an hour ago," she murmured: her hand lay on the child's hand.

"Stage fright," Lars offered.

"Don't say those things. He's my little boy."

"The family business! How many fathers, how many mothers, and presto, now a son—"

"I'm not like you." She stopped. "I'm not."

Again he gave her his impartial stare. "Dr. Eklund's not imaginary, no. That's the pity of it. I used to think he was."

"Neither is my mother. My mother's in Grenoble, with a new husband. I told you all that."

"It was a story."

"Some of it wasn't."

"Some of it! And after all this time you're ready to un-scramble it? The whole cast of characters?"

A gargantuan rumble obscured the last words. The child, awakened by his own vibration, drew up his legs, churned, and appeared to drop back into sleep. Two tracks of tears wandered down his chin—it was like the little stem of an acorn—and onto Elsa Vaz's sleeve: the hard-breathing nostrils wept, the fat lids watered.

"I shouldn't have come," she said.

"You shouldn't. Now that I see what you've come for."

"You don't see."

"A grand sorting-out. That high Party official, was *he* made up?"

"He was my mother's friend. I told you that. Tosiek Glowko."

"And the old widow with the box, and the old widower in Warsaw, and the shoes, and those papers in the oven, and the man with the long black coat—"

She looked at him; she was immobile. Even the pupils of her eyes stood stock-still. You could throw a pebble at them and they wouldn't twitch. "You don't know anything about Droho-bycz. Nothing. Nothing about Warsaw. It's all appetite to you—it's what you want it to be—you don't have any inkling about those places."

"I was born there. I'm a refugee."

"It doesn't matter how many times you say that, you still don't know where you were born. A fairy tale. You picked yourself a make-believe father out of a book. Who else does a thing like that—"

His steadiness faltered; he blinked: his own eye stung by that other eye. It was not so much a recollection as a smarting, a burning. That other eye would no longer submit to his sum-moning, even on the palest brink of memory. The truth was he could not call it back. When he tried to visualize it, what he saw was a very small mound of ash, irregularly round, no higher than a thumbnail. The gray cinders might have passed for a little heap of Elsa Vaz's hair.

"Tell me," he said, "is there a father for this boy somewhere? Or is he going to have to figure one out for himself?"

"His father is in Brazil."

"Brazil? Not Antwerp? He's escaped the family business?"

"Divorced" was what he thought he heard her say—the child's sick snore swelled up again and washed over it—but it might have been something else. It might have been "Forced," or "Lost," or "Crushed," or something similarly stretched out of her strangely middle-throated sound. It might have been anything at all; the moment passed; once more the child settled back.

Lars said resolutely, "You're the worst. You *named* yourself out of a book, I didn't do that. You swiped Adela, you dressed up in a name, you masqueraded—"

"Mrs. Eklund thought it would attract you. She wanted you to be interested."

"Mrs. Eklund. And the pupil, the schoolgirl? Copulation with a child! With one of his own pupils! That wasn't Mrs. Eklund's! That was yours, wasn't it—copulation with a child, wasn't that your idea? Heidi wouldn't think of that! I don't give her credit for that one."

"Give her credit if you like." She lowered her head. "I came to say you were abused."

"Used," he corrected.

"She injured you."

"And not Dr. Eklund? Dr. Eklund with his wonderful magnifying glass? Sherlock Holmes crossed with P. T. Barnum?"

"Not my father, no."

"Your father," he said vengefully.

"He injured you only a little."

"Thank you, only a little. I'm grateful."

"You injured him more. He isn't recovered. He'll never recover. You don't know what you did. That's why I'm here," she said. "I came to tell you what you did."

"What I did! I knocked out his handiwork. I suppose a thing like that can take an expert two or three months? Then it's all right, he can just go ahead and put together another one."

She said again, "You don't know what you did. You didn't know then and you don't know now."

"Well, if I knew, I'd be the expert, wouldn't I? I imagine it needs the right kind of ink, and the right kind of pen, and the right kind of paper, and the right kind of gullibility. I imagine he can get those things. And useful sorts of manuscripts—stray letters, smuggled correspondence—to model the handwriting on, that's the first. And after that a good storyteller like yourself—a natural Thespian I'd call you—and plenty of mishandling in the way that wrinkles up paper to make it age in a hurry, comings and goings in bags and jugs and maybe even shoes and ovens, and dunking in puddles—all that's technical, I don't know *how* it's done. But mainly it's having the right story that counts—it's the story, isn't it?"

"You literary parasites." She was all thick scorn; the boy stirred in her arms. She was a madonna of contempt. "Revenge and illusion, illusion and revenge! You think everything is imagination. There's more to the world than just imagination."

"Money," Lars suggested. "Isn't that what the family business is for?"

The boy shuddered; he was all at once awake. Heavily he lifted his acorn chin and looked sidelong around the cubicle. In the darkness of the doorway, upright on its haunches, a khaki mouse squatted. It was trembling all over. Its ears wavered; its whiskers shook; it held up its little paws like the hands of a child.

The boy cried out: a long shriek, and slipped to the floor.

"I've got to take him away."

"You shouldn't have brought him. A sick kid like that."

"What do *you* know about it?" The thickness of her scorn.

He felt she was right. It struck him—he thought of Karin's thrown-out paint set, Karin herself stolen away to America—it struck him that he had exchanged his daughter's hot life for a heap of gray ash. Illusion, illusion! And money. Wasn't he himself alive because of a mercenary traveler's family business in Warsaw long ago?

He said humbly, "I once had a child. She was taken away, I don't have her any more."

"Platonic. Literary." She didn't believe him, and why should she? It was himself saying it: a father-inventor can just as easily invent a child. "Isn't *any*thing of yours stuck in the here and now? You should ask yourself if *you* exist. Maybe you're only someone's theory. Someone's presupposition." She swooped up her little boy. "You lovers of literature. You parasites. That's why I came. To make sure you know."

She was without sympathy. He did not know what it was he was meant to know.

"You finished it off. Cremated. It's gone. The very one. The only one. It was what it was."

"Dr. Eklund's facsimile." How blurred; how weak.

"*The Messiah*," she pronounced: her face was locked; permanent; a live copper mold. "From Drohobycz. Via Warsaw. That one."

"It's you saying it," he said. "Adela says it. So much for that."

"Burned. Annihilated. Understand!" she commanded.

"You want to get even, that's why. The forger's daughter."

"It was what it was. He does passports, that's all. He can't do anything else. At least he's never tried. He gets people in and out, why don't you listen to Heidi? He can get people anywhere. My mother goes where she pleases. And so do I." She was, he saw, gathering herself up, along with her son. She was on her way, wherever that might be. "The last brainchild of Drohobycz," she told him, "gone up in smoke."

Thespian!

Refugee impostor!

He could not tell whether she would choose the elevator or the stairs. To his surprise, he heard a double clatter in the hollow of the stairwell, as rapid as a sewing-machine stitch: the boy's footsteps drumming after hers. She was without sympathy, why was that? She had the habit of obedience. She marched for her father. She was marching those little legs down.

It gave Lars as much time as he needed; he did not need much. He had forgotten which drawer of Nilsson's bruised old desk he had shoved it into. He splashed through one drawer after another—empty, nothing of worth in any of them. And there it was: the white beret, sticky with *Morgontörn* damp. He had carried it to the *Morgontörn* on the day after he left his old flat. The quilt was abandoned: heaped on the leather chair with its cracked leg, in the angle of the hallway.

He ran to the top of the stairwell—he could not see the mother or the child, but from the pattering stitches he understood that already they were close to the lowest landing.

"Mrs. Vaz!" he called into dim vertical air. "Your hat! Take back your hat!" and let it fall, spiraling, down and down and down.

17

NOT THAT he believed her. Now and then he discovered
that he did; mainly he did not.

What went on troubling him was the smell—that smell of
something roasting—all through Stockholm. It was a plague in
every corner of the city, no matter how cleanly the bright wind
came. Sometimes it seemed to lift from the baffled waters of the
locks; sometimes it steamed out of the tips of steeples. It always
found him out, wherever he was, whatever the season. It was as
if Stockholm, burning, was slowly turning into Africa: the smell,
winter or summer, of baking zebra.

He knew this was a hallucination—it was a sort of hallucination—Heidi would have insisted it was a hallucination—it was
a fancy. By the end of the year he had nearly stopped thinking
about the smell, except when he awoke in the morning; it was
always in his clothes in the morning.

The stewpot, for its part, had gone back to not taking much
notice of Lars Andemening: though his mail was gratifyingly
plentiful and Nilsson had added (despite the envious pallor of
Gunnar Hemlig and Anders Fiskyngel) a Sunday plum to his
Monday and his Tuesday.

Yet it happened on occasion—not very frequently—that

Lars grieved for his life. Not because he had failed to purify it. And not because of the lost *Messiah*. And not because he was an elderly orphan, and had put his finger into a dictionary to needle out a name. And not because of that perjured eye, thrown like a broken blind coal among the cinders of the brass amphora.

When, less and less often, the smell flushed up out of the morning's crevices, Lars inside the narrow hallway of his skull caught sight of the man in the long black coat, hurrying with a metal garter box squeezed under his arm, hurrying and hurrying toward the chimneys. And then, in the blue light of Stockholm, among zebra fumes, he grieved.

A NOTE ON THE TYPE

The text of this book was set on the Linotype in Fairfield, the first type face from the hand of the distinguished American artist and engraver Rudolph Ruzicka. In its structure Fairfield displays the sober and sane qualities of a master craftsman whose talent was long dedicated to clarity. It is this trait that accounts for the trim grace and virility, the spirited design and sensitive balance of this original type face.

Rudolph Ruzicka was born in Bohemia in 1883 and came to America in 1894. He designed and illustrated many books and created a considerable list of individual prints—wood engravings, line engravings on copper, and aquatints.

This book was composed by Maryland Linotype Composition Company, Baltimore, Maryland, and printed and bound by Fairfield Graphics, Fairfield, Pennsylvania.

Typography and binding design
by Dorothy Schmiderer